THE MAGE'S CURSE

BETHANY ADAMS

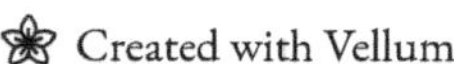 Created with Vellum

THE MAGE'S CURSE

Chalmys has the power to do nearly anything—except set himself free.

After a simple dinner with a god went very, very wrong, fae mage Chalmys was cursed to remain locked in his tiny realm. Until, that is, he could find someone to tell his story. All of his story.

There are only two problems: Revealing the truth of his birth will put his mother at grave risk, and he has to send his story through dreams.

Chalmys thought the second would be the easiest to overcome, but after centuries of tangled tales gone wrong, he has nearly given up hope. Until the night he connects with Holly. Now he has to convince her to risk everything to set him free. If only a certain god doesn't interfere...

CHAPTER 1

Chalmys gripped the edge of the table until his fingers ached. Fury and frustration scalded his blood, but he would gain nothing by snatching up the crystal hovering daintily in the stream of pure energy in front of him and tossing it against the wall. The clear, perfect stone had taken decades to find.

How many more decades could he bear to lose?

Shoving himself away from the table, Chalmys jerked to his feet and took a shaky breath before beginning his first circle of the room. The ancient wooden floor was worn thin from the centuries he'd paced here, tangible proof of his torment. Perhaps that was why he hadn't repaired the flaw even though it would require little magic. Not that he truly needed a reminder.

As he marched around the perimeter of the workroom, he did his best not to glance at the table in the center. He'd spent so much time creating the apparatus, from carving the sigils into the stone to meticulously channeling an entire ley line of energy through the center and connecting that line to the Earth dimension. A link that, with the aid of the crystal, allowed him to touch the minds of those in that far-flung land.

Sometimes.

Blasted humans. Over the centuries, they'd grown increasingly oblivious to the magic swirling around them. Most didn't believe in magic at all. If he lucked upon one with awakened fae blood, he could speak to them directly, but he only chanced to find one of those every generation or so. Although humans with dormant fae ancestry were more numerous, he could do little more but send them dreams and hope for the best.

And the only awakened part-fae he'd located in forty years had had the temerity to refuse his request. Why? The man could have done the task in a matter of months—certainly not more than a couple of years. It couldn't take that much effort to write down a tale given by another, but these humans—part fae or no—made it seem like a monumental task.

They weren't cursed to remain in this pocket dimension, though, were they? The god who'd consigned Chalmys to this fate had made it sound like an easy matter to break that curse, but clearly, it wasn't. *Only when another person can write your story will you be free.* Fine enough until he'd been bound so he couldn't leave his estate. Chalmys was only allowed to bring a person or two here every decade for a handful of months at a time.

He rarely tried that anymore, unless it was for companionship. Over the centuries, he'd begged, bargained, or—to his shame —forced a handful of bards and chroniclers to live here so they could recount his story when they returned to Earth. But none of them got the tale correct, at least not well enough to secure his release.

The fae-blooded he'd attempted to work through...their accounts were worse. His life was like a bad fairy tale. Powerful mage trapped by a curse, one seemingly simple task between him and freedom. But truth be told, no few of those Earth fairy tales *were* based in some way on him. Chalmys had sent his story through dreams, only to have the receiver morph him into a princess in a tower or a beast punished for pride.

In reality, he'd been punished for violating the codes of hospitality, but not by denying shelter to the weak or needy. This curse was all for a story—one it would have hurt his mother to tell. She'd been a priestess sworn to celibacy, for gods' sake. Her very soul could be forfeit if he shared that she'd borne him. Unfortunately, he hadn't been quick witted enough to come up with an alternative in time to please the god who'd demanded the tale of his birth.

If that was the only detail the chroniclers were missing, Chalmys was doomed. He would never betray his mother. But the wording of the curse hadn't been particularly specific. Chalmys eyed the crystal gleaming above the table in the center of the room. He had to keep trying. If he could find someone to get close enough to his full story, he could challenge the curse in front of the other gods.

He bound me to have my story told—he didn't say it must recount each and every moment.

With renewed determination, he returned to his seat. He flicked his finger, and the perfectly carved crystal octahedron spun in place. Slowly at first, but as soon as he joined his mind to both it and the ley line, the rotation picked up speed. Chalmys closed his eyes against the sight. He needed only his senses now.

Moonlight coated the clearing in silver and glinted against the golden threads embroidered in elaborate sigils along the hem of his opponent's robe. Kelth, who'd this very day attempted to enslave an entire village with his dark magic. It had taken most of the night to track the cur down, but he would finally pay.

"You're too honorable, Chalmys," the other mage said. "It'll come back to haunt you someday. Or perhaps this very night. Unlike you, I have no hesitation when it comes to killing."

Chalmys smiled coldly. "You forget the amount of justice I have delivered."

Smirking, Kelth waved his hand. "Against the weak."

Villains always considered themselves the smartest and strongest, and they had no comprehension of mercy. Magic was a gift, not a cudgel, but Chalmys was more than willing to use it as the latter when the ill-intentioned entered his territory. He did sometimes show mercy, and he made no attempt to stop the tales of such from spreading. They inevitably lulled the arrogant into complacency.

He marched closer, his robe snapping around his legs with each sharp step. This time—

Something wrapped around his wrist and pulled.

What...?

Holly woke with a gasp, and a cry stuttered in her throat as she was dragged abruptly to a new reality. Someone tugged hard at her arm. She'd just been preparing to do battle with an evil mage. Had she been transported here? What—

"Mama?"

What was she thinking? It must have been a dream.

Releasing a shaky breath, Holly turned her head until her daughter's worried face came into view. No mages. No clearing. Only Violet, who should still be tucked safely in her bed if the darkness was anything to judge by. Only the nightlight Holly kept for this very possibility allowed her to see her daughter at all.

"What's wrong, love?" Holly asked, her voice oddly rough.

Violet's fingers trembled against Holly's arm. "You yelled."

That would explain the hoarseness. "I'm sorry. I was having a bad dream."

Although when she stopped to think about it, the dream hadn't exactly been bad. Just...intense. So real. She could still feel the brush of thick, sumptuous fabric against her legs as she'd walked toward the mage. Except she hadn't been herself. Literally. She'd been a man. An angry, powerful man.

"Do you think that man is coming back?" Violet whispered before worrying her lower lip between her teeth.

For a moment, Holly thought she meant the evil mage or even

the male she'd been in her dream. Then reality hit. Violet wasn't worried about some wisp from her mother's sleeping brain. She was talking about her father, the very one who'd tried to blackmail Holly a week ago. The asshole who'd left her eight months pregnant and showed up from time to time only to ask for money—or custody.

Not that he really wanted the second one.

"I doubt it," Holly said, struggling to hide her anger. Of course Dylan would be back, but they'd have a few months or maybe a year, since she'd caved and given him the amount he'd demanded. "But if he does, I'll make him leave again."

Hopefully when Violet was at school or with the babysitter this time.

"Okay." Violet continued to bite at her lower lip, a sure sign that the questions weren't over. Not that they ever truly were when a five-year-old was involved. "Can I sleep with you? I'm scared."

Holly scooted over and patted the bed. "Hey, you'll be helping me out. I doubt any bad dreams will dare to come around when you're here."

Violet giggled. "I'm not scary."

"Oh, I don't know," Holly said as her daughter curled up on the mattress and tugged the blanket beneath her chin. "You can be pretty fierce when you want to be."

"Silly Mama."

With a smile, Holly kissed Violet on the top of her head and then gathered what was left of the blanket around her. She closed her eyes, hoping to return to sleep, but she couldn't manage it. All she could see was that mage, his handsome face twisted into a cruel sneer. Dream-her had practically pulsed with anger—but also confidence. Had he truly won the battle?

Ah, well. She rarely had the same dream twice, so she would never know.

CHALMYS RAN a shaky hand through his hair. He'd disconnected from the energy stream some time ago, but he couldn't make himself move. In all his centuries of confinement, such a thing had never happened. He'd sent countless dreams—countless—but none of the recipients had ever merged so closely that they saw the event through his eyes.

The woman's dormant fae blood wasn't particularly potent, but that hadn't mattered. Did she possess some talent that enabled her to live the memory? If so, she would be unique out of all those he'd sought aid from before. So uncanny. He didn't know what to make of it, but he knew one thing—it was dangerous.

How many of his thoughts and memories had she been able to glean during that brief merging? His secrets should be safe. She'd escaped from the dream before it was over, so he hadn't had the chance to implant the suggestion that she write what she'd seen down. Humans tended to dismiss such things. But if she had gained access to his deepest secrets, it would be foolhardy to work through her again.

And yet...

Perhaps the depth of their connection was a sign. Now that he knew of the possibility, he could attempt to control the strength of it, and if that worked, she might prove to be the one who set him free. Who better to tell his story than someone who could live it? There was potential within the danger.

Chalmys would have to tread carefully for so many reasons. Yes, there was his own safety—and his mother's. But his potential storyteller wasn't alone. The presence that had interrupted the dream had been a young one, resonant with energy like the woman's. Her child, perhaps? He was tempted to rejoin with the crystal for a quick scan to find out, but children were far too sensitive to magic to risk returning so soon.

That was for tomorrow night.

For now, he would be best served in researching the possible reasons for his strong connection to the woman. Some tome in his library surely held the secret to her unusual talent, and he might luck into a counter to it there. He could do a brief search before he sought his rest—if he even bothered to sleep.

There was far too much to uncover for that.

CHAPTER 2

*H*olly propped her chin on her hand and stared at the screen. Unfortunately, no matter how much she focused, the already jumbled mess of words only muddled further. Who in the world had translated this product manual, and how could any company have considered publishing it without a review by a native speaker? It was a good thing someone had bothered to read over it and hire her help before sending it out into the world.

Her eyelids drifted down for the hundredth time. This kind of challenge was usually a thrill—when Holly had more sleep. She'd spent far too many hours lying still and quiet in her bed fending off dream memories of evil mages and real memories of asshole exes. At this rate, it would take her an entire week to put this mess into order.

Despite that, Holly shoved away from her desk before she could fall asleep—again. She checked the clock on her desk. Not even noon. Violet wouldn't be out of school until nearly three, so if Holly set a couple of alarms, she could maybe get in a quick nap and still get a little work done. Better than trying to function like this.

After programming two alarms into her phone, Holly

stretched out on the couch and crammed the throw pillow beneath her head. She closed her eyes, expecting to drop into sleep almost at once. But no. Unexpected excitement thrummed through her blood. The mage she'd seen in her dream scared her, but the mage she'd *been* haunted her. Who was he? Would she ever know why her sleeping mind had conjured such people?

Expectation chased her into sleep.

CHALMYS PEERED into the crystal as though it held the secrets of the universe—or at least the answers to the questions he'd found in his library. As it turned out, there were very few reasons for the connection he'd shared with the woman last night. Either she was a particular kind of empathic bard...or she was his soulmate.

Gods help them all if it was the latter. That would allow her to know him better than anyone, it was true, but that didn't mean she would have the skill to create and share the actual story of his life. Certainly, he could bring her here as a companion—mate and wife. The gods would grant him that. But how could he trap someone else in this cursed existence? Not to mention that if the child he'd sensed was hers, that would be two affected.

Absolutely not.

The woman could be an empathic bard, however. He had no way of knowing after such short contact. He had to see what else he could discern about her, and she was unlikely to be asleep in the middle of the day. He wouldn't be able to communicate even through mental prompts, but he could skim her thoughts and glean more about her life.

He slipped into the crystal's power with a gentler touch than he'd used before. With less magic, it took a little more time to find her, but not as much as he might have expected. Her spirit shone like a ley line, and he was helpless to resist drawing near it. Shifting in his seat, he tried not to think about why.

Then he brushed her thoughts, and his breath caught. She'd fallen asleep. Not deeply, but it was a chance he hadn't anticipated having. She was so close to a dream state, too. Did he dare attempt to send another memory? Or should he try something better? He wouldn't normally be able to speak to her directly, but with their strong connection...

Before Chalmys had time to think better of it, he drew his awareness of himself closer and then projected himself into her thoughts. She would be able to see what he looked like. To speak to him. A risk, since it might frighten her if the effect was too strong.

But the centuries weren't getting any shorter.

MURKY SHAPES SURROUNDED Holly as she wandered along the nebulous ground. Nothing made sense. Not the soft mystery she stepped on nor the maybe-buildings at the edge of the gray mist. This wasn't like the clearing. That had been as focused and vivid as a fantasy movie. This place felt more like a dark, abandoned film set after the fog machine had been left on.

Then he appeared.

She halted, her gaze locking on the hottest man she'd ever seen standing just a few feet away. *Ungh.* His high cheekbones and firm, square jaw could have been carved by a master. And his full, kissable lips... She jerked her gaze away from his mouth before she embarrassed herself.

His shoulder-length, dark brown hair danced lightly across the rich green fabric of his robe as he tilted his head and studied her with open curiosity. A quick glance down confirmed that she was wearing jeans and a T-shirt. That had to seem as strange to him as his robes were to her.

Holly almost smacked her palm against her forehead at the thought. This was a dream, not reality. *He* wouldn't have a true opinion on anything.

"May I have your name?" the man asked.

Her breath caught. That voice. He sounded like... It was much like the voice from her last dream, except it had sounded deeper then, since she'd been the one speaking. Sort of. What was going on? She hadn't watched any fantasy shows lately. Maybe it was that D&D book she'd helped with a few months back. Her subconscious had clearly become obsessed with mages.

"I understand if you are hesitant," the man said, a reassuring smile crossing his lips, "But I would appreciate knowing what to call you."

Was this what people called lucid dreaming? There had to be a word for being aware you were dreaming while a figment of your imagination begged to know your name. Which you already knew. In your own mind, where dreams happen.

She shook her head at the strangeness of it all, but she answered anyway. "Holly."

His eyebrows shot up in surprise. "An apt moniker. I would add holly to a dream-enhancing tincture."

A tincture? Was he serious? She must have eaten something strange for breakfast, because she couldn't think of another reasonable explanation for her brain to create this odd encounter. She hadn't had alcohol in ages, wasn't on medication, and didn't do drugs. Not with Violet to take care of.

"I feel like someone slipped me some kind of enhancement, but not one for dreams," she muttered.

"Truly?"

In a few long strides, the mage reached her, and the concern on his face sent an odd warmth to her heart even as she wanted to laugh at the misunderstanding. Then she peered at him more closely, and the chuckle stalled in her throat. Aquamarine and amber danced together in his eyes, a color far beyond mere hazel, and there was a strength and timeless confidence within those depths that she'd never seen.

Holly expelled a sharp but shaky breath. "No. I was being

sarcastic. I mean…I'm asleep. None of this is real. How did I even come up with this stuff?"

"Hmm." The wry curve of his full lips sent her heart racing. "Are you a bard, Holly?"

Yet another odd question. Tinctures and bards. She pinched the bridge of her nose. What else? "I'm a technical writer and editor. If you need a how-to guide, I'm your woman. I haven't written fiction in ages."

His forehead creased. "You've lived ages? With your fae blood unawakened?"

Cereal. She'd had cereal for breakfast, and the milk hadn't tasted off. Maybe someone at the factory had added more than sugar with the oats? "There has to be a way to get yourself out of a lucid dream."

"What if this isn't a dream?" the man asked. "I am Chalmys, a mage of great power, and I seek someone who can tell my story."

Did her subconscious want her to write a book? Hah. "I don't have time for that."

"It surely cannot take much effort to transcribe my life."

Well, that was just rude. Now her own brain was devaluing her work. "I can translate jargon into a manual pretty quickly, but a book is something else entirely. No one will read a story that's a dry list of events. Good writing takes time, at least for me, and I have a daughter to support. Messing around with some dream story won't pay the bills."

"I didn't—"

Clang.

The sound of bells reverberated through the clearing, and the mists around them roiled into a frenzy. Chalmys stepped back, his form fading in and out of her sight. She almost reached out before she stopped herself. The bells could mean anything. A warning, maybe. Before she could decide, her world tilted as she was pulled from the clearing.

Into her sunny living room and the loud, insistent droning of her alarm.

With a groan, Chalmys dropped his forehead against his palm.

Good writing takes time, at least for me, and I have a daughter to support. Messing around with some dream story won't pay the bills.

She'd laid bare his greatest obstacles in only a couple of sharp sentences—and not just with her. He'd always assumed that a decent bard could write down the dreams he sent and then go on with the rest of their work for the day. They didn't have to create what happened, so what was the problem? But Holly was correct. For his tale to be read and known, it would have to be both accurate *and* compelling. Rushing or cheapening the process had only led to tales of princesses in towers or epic mage battles with no other substance.

For Holly to accept this task and do it justice, she would have to neglect her obligation to her daughter. That would never do. Had he the good fortune to have a child, he would not leave them wanting to pursue some mage's random fancy. The idea was obscene. He would have to find another way, even if it meant searching for another to connect with.

Of course, he could offer payment, but it would take some work. His magic was bound by the curse to be largely contained to this place, though most of that was a side effect rather than a direct punishment—it required a strong shield to prevent him from breaking free. However, he'd found ways around the obstacle. He would need a few days to prepare the various spell components and gather the requisite amount of gold to send her.

But what did he have if not time?

CHAPTER 3

*A*s soon as Holly pressed send on the email, the now-familiar restlessness beat at her until she tapped her fingernails against the keyboard. She'd managed to keep the worst of the antsy feeling at bay while completing the product manual, but now that that project was on its way back to the client, she'd lost her diversion. She hadn't received the file for her next job, either.

Five days. Five days had passed since the weird mage dreams, but she couldn't forget them. She'd even started a file to type out what had happened, but she couldn't get her fingers to dump the memories onto the page. What would be the point? She really couldn't spare the time it would take to write an entire book, and then she'd have to use up even *more* time to figure out how to publish the thing. If it turned out to be worth showing to anyone.

She had a million reasons to forget the silky, tempting voice of the gem-eyed mage as he'd spoken of his need for a bard. A bard, of all things. And her number one reason only had a couple of weeks before school let out for the summer, which meant Holly would have to juggle her work even more carefully. Fake dream men couldn't be a temptation.

How long had it been since she'd had sex, anyway? Because,

seriously, she was beyond desperate if she was getting obsessed with a figment of her own imagination. *Of course* she'd created the hottest man she'd ever seen. She hadn't had a date in...hell, who knew? Maybe it was time to find a babysitter and have a night out with her friends. Anything to increase the chances of meeting a real person to date.

Huffing at the turn of her thoughts, Holly closed her laptop and headed for the front door. The sun gleamed down from a bright blue sky, an unseasonably cool breeze brushed through the trees, and she had a couple of hours until Violet got home. A nice walk around the neighborhood would be just the thing. By the time she returned home, hopefully her latest client would have emailed her what she needed for the next project.

When she found herself comparing the sky to the glowing turquoise of her dream mage's eyes, she pressed her lips firmly together and told her brain to shut the hell up.

THIS TIME, Chalmys stood within the elaborate stone circle situated where his gardens met up with the forest. He'd parted the soil and lifted the bedrock to surface level, creating a living floor connected to the earth's heart. He'd spent nearly a month carefully smoothing the stone and then carving each sigil he'd need for his spells.

He could do magic without this kind of circle, but it took far more effort and personal power that way. Here, he could set up and maintain multiple spells simultaneously, which was exactly what he needed today. This trick would require few of his personal energy reserves with the circle's use.

Chalmys dropped the pouch of gold coins into the center with a muffled clink and walked to the northernmost point of the circle. The sigils here aided in stability, balance, and grounding—a base point for any working. He removed a crystal from his pocket and settled it into the niche above the first sigil. Then with a quick stretch of his power, he activated the spell he'd prepared.

Golden light flared as the magic spread from symbol to symbol until every delicate carving appeared lit from within. A ring of light formed at the edge of the stone and flared upward until it met in a dome above, and the rock beneath his feet tingled with the power of the base he'd created. He probed the construction carefully but found no sign of a flaw.

Excellent.

Chalmys moved around the circle, selecting and installing more crystals in their requisite places. One to the east that brought his thoughts into almost painful clarity, one to the south to create the brief breach in the shield, and two in the west to aid in the transfer of the pouch. But for the last, a crystal octahedron like the one in his workroom, he connected the other spells into a nexus point in the center and hovered the crystal there, just above the pouch of gold.

All he had to do now was connect that nexus point into the same ley line he used to reach Earth. From there, he would have to work fast. The shielding that enclosed him here acted quickly to reseal any hole he made, which he'd learned the hard way the first few times he'd tried to bring in supplies. That had gone so poorly that he'd petitioned the council of gods for aid and now had most things delivered to him by their magic. Only the odd thing required this level of effort.

If fortune favored him, it would prove worthwhile.

Chalmys closed his eyes, lifted his hand, and wove the nexus into the ley line with a few deft twists. The spell embedded into the octahedron flared to life, flashing light against his closed eyelids, but he ignored the harsh glow. In only a heartbeat—yes, there. The magic latched onto the pouch as the southern crystal burned the path through. He found Holly's tiny estate, and with a twist of his finger, sent the pouch to land atop a paper-covered desk.

No sound came through—no clatter of gold to confirm its

safe landing. Chalmys glimpsed the spot for only a moment to check before dropping the link to her home. Then he unwound the spells as quickly as he'd activated them. He did this periodically if he needed something unusual for his work, but it was best not to linger and risk drawing the gods' attention to his work. Especially from the one who'd bound him.

With the gold delivered, Chalmys would seek Holly in her dreams tonight, and there he would make his offer. What she would make of the gold in the meantime he could only guess, but there was nothing he could do about that now. Hopefully, the vague note he'd dared to leave inside would prevent her from acting hastily.

Alas...humans were difficult to predict.

HOLLY'S MOOD was as light as the sunshine as she unlocked the front door and stepped through. It wasn't just because of the beautiful day, either. Her phone had pinged with three new emails along the way, one of them with the files she needed and two others with new jobs. Technical writing paid the bills, but there was always the risk of work drying up. Any day with new offers was a good day.

Pleasure hummed through her so steadily that she'd already sat down before she noticed the brown leather pouch slumped amidst the papers on her desk. Holly sucked in a breath. What the hell? She hadn't left this here. She didn't even *own* anything like this. Had someone broken into her house?

She shoved away from the desk and grabbed the baseball bat she kept tucked underneath. They didn't live in a bad neighborhood, but crime could happen anywhere. Like here. Today. Though she'd told herself it paid to be safe as a single mom, she'd still snickered at herself when she'd placed the bat in the back corner under the desk where her feet didn't reach. *Take that, past me.*

Her throat went dry, but her fingers tightened around the smooth wood until her hands stung as she lifted the baseball bat and crept toward the hall. If someone was still in here, they were going to regret their poor life choices. She'd played baseball with her brothers for years and could swing like a champ.

Hell, if she pretended the intruder was Dylan, it would be even easier to beat the shit out of them.

But as she checked each room, including closets, and verified that all windows and doors were locked, her resolve gave way to the knot of fear throbbing in her chest. She even pulled down the steps to the attic and searched up there. Nothing. No one was here, and there was no sign that anyone had been, except her and Violet.

The bat hung loosely in her hand as she approached the desk once more. How could something just...appear? It didn't make any sense. Unless Violet had brought it home from school yesterday? Maybe a few of the papers had been on it, and a breeze from the opening door had moved them. Or something.

That or she really did need to buy a new brand of cereal. First weird dreams, and now hallucinations.

Fingers trembling, Holly nudged the bag before jerking her hand away like a goofball. It was a little leather pouch, not a bomb. Even so, she had to fight the temptation to smack it with the baseball bat. If it held something special to Violet, that wouldn't go over well. Not if she crushed whatever was inside.

"Just open the bag," Holly muttered to herself.

After a ridiculously long pep talk, she sat back down and snatched the pouch up in one resolved swoop. It was oddly weighty. Nibbling at her lower lip, Holly hefted the bag in her palm. Marbles? Rocks? Violet did like to collect pretty stones. But there was only one way to know for sure. She untied the leather cords holding the pouch shut, took a deep breath, and parted the opening before she could second-guess herself.

She peered over the lip like Pandora peeking into her troublesome box, but best she could tell, no horrors sprang free. The shadowed shapes in the bottom of the bag did look like they might be rocks, but without more direct light, it was impossible to tell what kind. Curious now, Holly tipped the pouch over her desk and spilled the contents across her papers.

A beam of sunshine caught against gold as the stones settled in a jumbled pile, a small, rolled piece of paper sticking out of the top. Holly blinked, then blinked again. These weren't rocks from the yard. These were actual, honest-to-God pieces of gold. She pinched the nearest one and lifted it close.

Not just gold—coins.

Holly stared at the delicate pattern of leaves stamped into the side. Her daughter couldn't have left this. Pressing her free hand against her sternum, Holly flipped the coin over. This time, there was a woman's image. A queen, based on the crown atop her head. The lady's head was turned as though she was looking at something next to the artist who'd rendered the depiction—not quite a full profile but close. Because of that, Holly could make out the point of the queen's ear, much like a fairy or an elf.

The coin slipped out of her suddenly numb fingers as she scrambled to make meaning out of the impossible. There had to be a rational explanation, right? She stared at the roll of paper sticking from the pile like a little flag. Maybe this was a prank, or a toy, or a prop from a play, and the paper had info about the owner or manufacturer. She'd helped write little inserts like that. She could read this one and then have a good laugh at the perfectly logical, totally sane reason for a pouch of gold to be in her house.

Her hands shook as she unrolled the paper and flattened it against her desk. Was it in English? She blinked, and what she'd thought were squiggles resolved into readable text. A nervous laugh slipped through Holly's lips. Yep. It had totally been that way the whole time. Completely understandable English.

I have considered your words, and you are correct. You deserve recompense. Please accept this gold in payment for your consideration. I would provide double that upon completion of the project.
Chalmys

This time the laughter was no small slip—more a choked, hysterical tumble. Either she'd fallen asleep without realizing it, or she was developing a new mental illness. Holly had only heard that name one other time in her life—during her dream. She'd never told anyone the details of that, not even Violet. No one could have known about the dream mage who'd asked Holly to write his story.

She did her best to slow her breathing even as she scooped the coins and paper back in the pouch and tied it tight. Everything would be okay. Either she would wake up soon and swear off cereal, or she would make an appointment with her therapist. Maybe both. There wasn't any shame in needing help. It could just be the stress of dealing with Dylan.

But deep inside, she couldn't shake the feeling that this was all too real.

CHAPTER 4

*A*lthough she'd shoved the pouch of gold to the back of her desk drawer, Holly hadn't been able to shake it from her thoughts. Not as she'd met Violet at the school bus or as she'd cooked dinner. Not as she'd listened to her daughter's stories about school—and definitely not as she'd washed the dishes. Everywhere, that sunshine glint haunted her thoughts, the serene face of that mysterious fae queen sticking with her like a ghost.

What could it mean? Could her dream man—hah—really exist? How could gold just appear?

"Did that man come back, Mama?"

Violet's worried question jerked Holly from her rambling thoughts with a quickness, but it took her a moment to realize that her daughter wasn't talking about the mysterious Chalmys. She hoped. "The one who scared you? No."

"You look worried like that day." Her face still pink from her bath, Violet shifted on her feet beside her unicorn-themed bed. "So I thought maybe..."

"Oh, sweetie, I'm sorry." Holly sank down onto the edge of the mattress and pulled her daughter into a hug. "It was just a weird day, that's all. Have you been worrying about him all this time? I've known that man a long time. He's annoying but not dangerous."

Violet snuggled against her neck for a moment, but when she leaned back, a worried little frown knit her brows. "Is he my daddy?"

"No!" Holly objected at once, the tight, strangled sound of her voice making Violet flinch. Holly took a deep breath and forced herself to calm. "I'm sorry," she murmured. Again. "It's complicated."

Her daughter's frown deepened. "I heard him say something about custody, and that sounded like cussing, and that's bad. But I asked Mrs. Wilkins if custody was the same as bad words, and she said it meant a grownup who was in charge of a kid, like a mommy or daddy or guardian. But not a guardian angel. I made sure. So I thought he had to be one of those. Except the angel."

Normally, Violet's mad rush of words made her smile, but not these words. Her shoulders slumped. She'd done her best to keep Dylan from meeting their daughter, but of course, he'd wrecked that, too. "Listen. Dylan is...technically, he's your father, but he ran away before you were born. He's not your daddy, though. A daddy loves you and cares for you no matter what."

"How do I get one?"

The calculating glint in her daughter's eyes made Holly uneasy. "Well. If I ever find a man I like and he likes us... Well, maybe we could make a new family. The best families want to be together, after all. A real daddy is there for you always."

And not for money, but Holly didn't say that part aloud. Violet was barely ready for what she'd already learned. She wouldn't understand the full situation. If Holly had a choice, her daughter would never have to know about it at all, but that was a wish unlikely to come true, especially with Dylan getting bolder.

"Okay," Violet said before crawling to the center of her bed and burrowing beneath her covers. "Then we'll wait to find a good one. I don't really need anyone else, anyway."

Holly's heart went soft and melty at the sweet words. "I don't either, baby. But I do need to read you a bedtime story."

Contentment replaced the unsettled feeling of earlier as she sat beside Violet with her chosen story and read until her daughter drifted off to sleep. It was an easy night—a peaceful one. There were others when it took forever to get Violet calmed down and tucked in, but she must have worn herself out with worry over her fears about Dylan.

Violet was a naturally cheerful child, but even she had her limits.

By the time Chalmys sat down in his workroom later that night, his mood had landed somewhere between excited and nervous. He had no idea what she'd thought of his offer. He hadn't scried to determine Holly's reaction, not after using so much energy transporting the gold to her domain. Doing so immediately following that kind of magic might have drawn suspicion if his captor had decided to look.

As the moon crept high into the sky, Chalmys gathered his composure. She would accept or she would not. He had to be prepared for either and not lose his focus. He wanted to enter into her dreams directly again, a feat that required intense concentration, and time to speak to her was not guaranteed. She could be drawn from her sleep as she had been before. The longer he could maintain his own control, the better.

Chalmys linked with the crystal floating above his worktable, and the stone spun ever faster until it blurred before his eyes. He didn't need to see it. As easily as breathing, he slipped into the line of power and followed it to the now-familiar home of the woman who so intrigued him. He fell into her dreams in a matter of moments, manifesting himself as he had before.

This time, however, he sent her the image of a forest—the ancient one near his estate, to be exact. It felt natural for his spirit to walk here as he projected his true form for her to see, and if he were lucky, she would not be so suspicious outside of the nebulous mists he'd thought to use before. That place might have been void of distractions, but he hadn't missed the glint of fear in her green eyes as she'd glanced around them.

Between one breath and the next, she appeared. Holly. Her nut-brown hair tangled around her shoulders a bit haphazardly, and the soft-looking, striped clothing she wore reminded him of bedclothes. He couldn't help but smile. She didn't know how to control the image of herself that she projected into the dream, that much was clear.

There was a different kind of wariness to her steps this time. Before, she'd glanced around her with fear, advancing as slowly as anyone in a new environment would. This time, her eyes were on him, and there was an awareness there that felt more...personal. Her hesitant approach, the wariness lining her face—those were for him, not the dream forest.

She halted just out of reach. "This can't be real," she said at once.

He noted the pallor beneath her lightly tanned skin. Fear, also for him. "Can't it?"

"Tell me something I couldn't have dreamed." Her lips turned down. "Though if this is all in my head, I suppose that's impossible."

"Perhaps. Or perhaps not," he said. "Give me a moment to think?"

At her slight nod, Chalmys cast a portion of himself free, back into the ley line's energy. What could he offer that she didn't already know? He was no seer to foretell the future, or he never would have fallen into his current trap. Something she hadn't noted in her home, maybe? He scried through her house, but nothing stood out.

Then a soft whimper caught his attention. Her daughter. The child cried out softly in her sleep, and her thoughts swirled around him so strongly he only had to scry for what she projected to understand why. A bad dream, and a distinctive one. Were she an adult, Chalmys might have delved into her mind and spelled her to remember the nightmare to make the proof more certain, but he would do no such thing to a child.

Chalmys retreated fully back into himself and then opened his eyes. "There is a man who scares your daughter. She dreams of him appearing at her school."

Holly gasped, her shoulders going tense. "My daughter is not involved in...whatever this is. If this is more than a dream, you'd better not be messing with her."

"I do not meddle in the minds of children. Ever," he said sharply, unable to prevent his tone from chilling. "I did not enter her dreams. She projected them, and I gleaned the images from the energy around her. Children are sacrosanct."

For one long moment, Holly studied him, no sign of softening on her face. Then the tension leeched from her shoulders, and she sighed. "I can't even prove this part until I wake up."

His robes rustled with his shrug. "I am no seer. Even were I to scry some detail from your environment, you would have no way to prove you hadn't seen it before. Our minds store many facts."

"This is impossible." She rubbed her palm against her brow. "All of it."

If only he could ease the troubled, lost expression on her face. Suddenly, he wanted to brush the tumble of her hair back and caress her soft cheek, but she wouldn't accept his comfort. They were too much strangers for any such thing.

"My offer of gold is real," Chalmys said. "And I truly do need your help. I am trapped. Cursed to remain locked away unless I can find someone who can tell my story. I've lost count of the years spent searching through dreams for anyone capable of completing this task. But you were right to point out your own dilemma. Your effort has value."

The choked sound she made could almost be called a muffled laugh—if he were feeling creative. "You do realize that I can't use those coins, right? No one pays for things with gold anymore.

Not anyone I know, at least. I can't even sell them for the metal's value. How could I explain the images stamped on the coins? It would be really suspicious."

He frowned. He hadn't considered complications in her world. "What do the images matter?"

"There are people who collect coins from ancient civilizations," Holly explained. "But I'm pretty sure none of those civilizations had fae queens stamped on them. If I took them to a collector, they'd ask where I found them. I don't know, maybe a jewelry store would buy the coins for the metal, but I have no idea what to say when they ask for details."

Chalmys crossed his arms and tapped his finger against his chin. This was a dilemma. If human forms of payment had shifted so heavily, then it would take time to research proper compensation. Of course, he had time—nothing but. Yet he had no time at all, for the lonely misery of his exile strangled around him more with each passing day.

"I do not know what to offer," he admitted.

Two tiny lines formed between her eyebrows as she peered at him. "I can't decide if this is real or if I'm going crazy. The look on your face says truth, but it's impossible."

"Is it, then?" He dropped his arms and took a step closer. "I wish you were correct. I wish I could open my eyes and find myself free. Instead, I'm doomed to merely exist, all for a single misstep in service of another."

She sighed. "This sounds like a ridiculous fairy tale."

"Tell that to the god who cursed me," Chalmys snapped before thinking better of the words. "Or rather, don't. I would not see you equally burdened by his displeasure."

"If all of this is true, I can't be the first person you've asked."

"Oh, no." His hands clenched into fists. "I've spent centuries on this quest. Unfortunately, no one interprets the dreams correctly. Or if they see them clearly, they embellish the story for their own pleasure. I need a true account."

Holly stared at him. "Centuries?"

Chalmys nearly cursed. Had he scared her away with that detail? He had to hope not.

He wasn't certain he could hold out much longer.

WHY IN THE world did she find herself believing him? Had stress finally pushed her into delusion? Except...there was a crispness to this dream she'd never experienced before. And she rarely dreamed the same thing twice, much less carried on debates with the same person. Then there was the gold. She'd held those coins in her own two hands.

He claimed to have searched for centuries, and though the thought had left her stunned for a moment, it made perfect sense. He had to be some kind of fae or fairy or elf. And didn't that just match the way he'd tried to pay her? Even without the image stamped on the coin, the pouch of gold was such a fae thing to offer.

But the fairy stories she'd read in college hadn't mentioned a cursed mage. Had they? Chalmys claimed that all other attempts had gone wrong. Any number of tales could have been based on him, but she couldn't recall any particularly close to this.

Ugh. What was she thinking? How could she simply accept something so ridiculous?

"Perhaps I should not have given my age," Chalmys grumbled.

Holly lifted a brow. "You didn't. That was barely a hint."

"One hint more than I should have given."

At the sight of his self-castigating frown, she chuckled. Maybe he *was* a figment of her imagination, because it would be pretty typical of her to get annoyed after telling herself information she didn't want herself to know. She debated her own decisions often enough while awake.

"So you've inspired some stories," Holly said. "I would ask you which ones, but that wouldn't be hard for dream-me to fill in."

Chalmys rubbed his finger against his chin. "Try *Østenfor sol og vestenfor mane.*"

A chill raced over her skin. "What? What language is that?"

"I hardly know," he answered with a shrug. "I've learned countless tongues through magic, but I have no idea what they'd be called in your language. A bit of nonsense, that. Shouldn't a language or country be called by the name it gives itself?"

Holly couldn't refute his words, since she'd wondered about that very thing herself. España wasn't more difficult to say than Spain, but English-speakers changed it nonetheless. And why Japan instead of Nihon? Had her ancestors gone around calling places whatever they wanted just for the hell of it? Some names might be harder to pronounce than others, but they clearly hadn't even tried.

"Holly?"

She shook herself free from her thoughts with a blush. "Sorry. Anyway. I'm never going to remember that title, much less figure out how to spell it. But it's okay. Since you can't pay me and I won't work for free, it doesn't really matter."

His eyes widened, and the cool confidence he wore as easily as his robe suddenly wavered. "Wait. Don't say no yet. The thought of beginning this search again without a hint of hope... Please. There must be some way I can pay you. If not coins, are there goods you could more easily sell?"

Holly almost waved him off like the dream he surely was, but the hint of panic pinching his brows gave her pause. If there was the slightest possibility this was true, then how could she deny him out of hand? Could she bear the thought of some poor man trapped all alone in another dimension while she went on about her life without a care?

Okay, not without a care—she was a self-employed single mom, after all. But still.

No, she couldn't dismiss him. Not without trying to help. How *could* he pay her, though? What kind of things did people receive out of nowhere? An inheritance? A rare yard sale find?

Either of those excuses would work, so long as the items didn't look like stuff she'd stolen from a fairy castle.

"What about old jewelry?" Holly ventured. "The kind of stuff that might be in your grandmother's jewelry box?"

Chalmys's lips twitched. "Lest I make another mistake, I should warn you that my grandmother had an entire room dedicated to her filigreed tiara collection."

"Of course she did." Holly pressed the heel of her palm between her eyes. "I suppose *old* jewelry has a different meaning for you, too, Mr. Centuries. A bad suggestion all around. But… how much of my world can you observe? A quick look around antique stores should give you an idea, so long as you don't pick the rarest or most expensive things as your model."

"Noted," Chalmys said, dipping his head in acknowledgement. "I will observe as you suggested and shape the gold into something more suitable. Give me a week? I'll leave a new pouch on your desk while your child is not present."

A chill rushed over Holly's skin, and she rubbed her upper arms in a vain attempt to warm them. How could she be so cold in a dream? "I suppose it'll prove whether this is real."

Chalmys gripped her shoulders just above where her own hands rested. "Good luck retrieving your bed coverings."

"Huh?" Heat speared through her from his touch, but she couldn't stop puzzling over his words. Why was he suddenly talking about covers? "We're standing in a forest. How could I have—"

"*Mama!*"

And just like that, both dream and man were gone.

CHAPTER 5

To Holly's chagrin, Chalmys had been right about the bed covers. Violet's voice might have pulled her from the dream, but it was her body that had claimed most of the blanket before Holly had managed to wake. Seeing the fear in her daughter's eyes, though, she hadn't complained. Instead, she'd tucked the blanket more firmly around her little girl and sang softly until the child was back asleep.

It was almost summer, but the forecast had called for a surprisingly cool night. She'd meant to turn the thermostat up before bed, too. Even if the heat hadn't kicked on, it wouldn't have been so cold to start with. Too bad she'd been so preoccupied. Now, she was left to shiver beneath her thin sheet and ponder her newest dream.

By all rights, she should dismiss it. She'd been under a lot of stress, especially with Dylan popping up so unexpectedly. She already had a bad feeling about *that*. In all the time since Violet had been born, he'd only texted her to arrange for money. He didn't want even the illusion of being a father, or so he'd always claimed. So to show up threatening custody...?

It wasn't good.

Holly could so easily wave away her dream as some kind of

manifestation of her worry. She *did* feel trapped by Dylan and his demands. Yet she couldn't. There was a clarity to each dream featuring Chalmys that she'd never experienced before. For one thing, each one had made sense. What dream made sense from start to finish? Even the first one, where she'd seen everything from the mage's eyes, had been logical.

Usually, her dreams were disjointed. One scene would morph into something different, or people she hadn't seen in years would show up. Maybe the room would be upside down. Or strange creatures would appear. Once, she'd been brushing her teeth with hair gel while a lemur swung from the light fixture, at least until her great-grandmother had rushed in to take the lemur back to the office for a business meeting.

She'd never met her great-grandmother, and as far as she knew, no lemurs worked in offices. But she *had* gone to the zoo earlier in the day, and she'd fallen asleep watching a historical drama featuring an actress who looked suspiciously like the woman in her dream. Really, only the hair gel was a mystery in that one.

Those experiences with Chalmys? She'd had full, consistent conversations with him. Yeah, the topics were technically odd, but they made sense—especially if he *was* a trapped mage. Even that strange place with the fog where they'd first spoken had looked real, no morphing into something else. She really might have been transported there by some strange magic.

Ah, what was she thinking? If there was any real magic in the world, she could have put up a force field against Dylan. Surely, some wizard would have ejected him into the stratosphere. Or banished him to a deserted island. Or sent him to jail for extortion. A fairy godmother would've come to save her, at the very least. The fates wouldn't be so unkind as to send her a helpless mage who thought a writer's work had no value.

Or...that was exactly what they would do.

Damn.

WITH NO SMALL amount of curiosity, Chalmys scried past yet another long strip of shops. The humans so frequently changed their world, a phenomenon that had both attracted him and prevented him from looking at it too closely. Lately, he'd avoided doing more than scrying for people with fae blood. The sight of so many new places he couldn't visit and so many novel inventions he couldn't explore sent a spike of pain directly into his heart.

Though some inventions were more bother than joy—like money.

There'd been some form of currency for centuries, of course. But the inability to easily trade valuable resources for goods? That was new. Worse, his search had revealed that many items were purchased with rectangular cards. Or small, handheld computers waved over a box. When had humans made the leap from large box computers with ugly, monochrome screens to...that? This new kind fit in pockets.

Obviously, he had grown too out of touch with the human world. It would be best to follow Holly's advice with care, and that meant focusing on antique shops only. So he ignored the stores advertising phones or clothes or home décor, sending his awareness ever onward in search of an appropriate antique jewelry store.

Nothing too rare or fancy, she'd said. Something a human might see in their grandmother's jewelry box. Chalmys sighed. Perhaps his first step should have been searching for grandmothers with jewelry boxes. He hadn't known his mother's mother, and his father's... She'd been born of a marriage between Iperan—his realm's god of metalworking—and the fae queen stamped on the coins he'd given Holly.

Needless to say, his concept of what was typical was...skewed.

He hadn't been exaggerating about the room of filigreed tiaras. His grandmother was the queen now, and her father still showered her in his creations. Not that Chalmys knew how she felt about the extravagance. He had only been in the palace while training with the court mages, and he'd only seen the room while studying one of the spells used to secure it. Prince Kleress might have been shameless enough to seduce a priestess, but he'd at least had the decency not to acknowledge the son born of that union. Did the queen know? Did her father, Iperan? It would explain the boons Chalmys had been granted by the council of gods, but he certainly wasn't going to ask.

Finally, he spotted a store that seemed decent enough. Clean, well-kept, and brightly lit, with glass displays along the walls and in an oval in the middle. There'd been a couple of posh stores boasting the kind of jewelry a fae noble might wear—those places were the haunt of rich human grandmothers, no doubt—but these displays held simpler designs with fewer precious gems. In a few cases, there were even duplicates, which suggested this store was less likely to deal in the one-of-a-kind.

He took his time studying each display. Sunlight shifted angles through the window as hours passed, and humans came and went from his awareness like bees wandering the garden. One or two even sensed him. When their brows scrunched and their eyes lifted to search the air, Chalmys pulled his energy farther away, though only after a quick mental probe. Each had traces of fae blood, but none were strong enough for him to slip into their dreams.

By the time he'd seen enough to return to himself, sweat coated his brow and his muscles trembled with fatigue. Between holding the dream space for Holly and spending hours exploring Earth, even his vast energy was somewhat depleted. Perhaps it was time he finally rested. He'd noted several gold necklaces and bracelets he could easily recreate when he woke.

If he'd received any benefit from his father's line, it was the ability to work with metal and gems. Not with the skill of a god, but that would have been a hindrance, anyway. Holly would never be able to sell something created by Iperan without causing a stir. But a few pieces of elegant jewelry? That Chalmys could do.

SOMEHOW, Holly had managed to get a bit of work done, but by dinner, her nerves were as frayed as the cheese she was vigorously grating. A week. The mage had requested a week to send her this new payment, and she had foolishly agreed. Now, she had seven days of waiting before she learned if her dreams were real.

Though it made her question her sanity a little, she couldn't help but ponder what he might create. A mage who could slip into dreams was obviously powerful, but that didn't mean he could fashion jewelry with any skill. Which might be a good thing. If the designs were too beautiful, she would want to keep the pieces instead of selling them.

Anyway, where *could* she sell jewelry? There was always the internet, of course, but a local shop might give her a better deal. Maybe. She'd been rather spontaneous in her suggestion for a woman who'd never inherited anything of value. A grandmother's jewelry box. What would she know of that? Her grandparents had all died before she was born. Which meant she needed to spend quality time on her computer researching antique shops, or she'd end up no better off than she'd been with the gold coins.

If what Chalmys gave her was legit. She could always end up with nothing.

Pain seared her thumb.

"Ow!" she yelped as she bent down to peer at her skin.

A thin line of red welled up on the side of her thumb from where it had caught against the grater, and the block of cheese she held was now a nub. Muttering curse words, Holly jerked her hands away from the bowl before blood could drip on the ridiculously large pile of cheese. Good thing she'd already planned to add more than the recipe's suggested cup.

Maybe not this much more, but whatever.

After setting the grater by the sink, she grabbed the first aid kit and took care of the scratch. It was the small-but-annoying kind, the sort of cut that would make typing painful for the foreseeable future. How could she have been so careless? She knew better than to let her mind drift during such a task.

She peeked across the kitchen to the dining area, where Violet sat at the table. She still wore her headphones, thankfully—otherwise, Holly would have received quite a lecture about saying bad words. For once, she was saved by homework. Violet loved that reading app so much that she usually played longer than the assigned twenty minutes.

More carefully, Holly grabbed a pan and cooked the beef for the taco casserole. Since it was her mom's recipe and a family favorite, she was familiar enough with it to move on autopilot. That made it difficult to keep her thoughts from wandering in the process, but she managed to arrange everything in the casserole dish, complete with extra cheese, and pop it in the oven without hurting herself again.

Really, it was the most contentious cooking session she'd ever had—which was especially embarrassing since she'd been fighting with herself. Thoughts of Chalmys had circled around the perimeter of her mind, forcing her to shove them away constantly. Tired, Holly leaned against the counter and let out a long sigh.

Her phone vibrated against her hip, and her heart gave a little leap. *Chalmys?* Wait, why had she thought of his name? As she tugged the phone from her pocket, heat rushed into her face. She was in trouble if her subconscious anticipated a text from a dream mage. Seriously. Even if he *were* real, he wouldn't have this kind of technology. Otherwise, he would just call.

She tapped to open the text, then froze. It was from Dylan: *I need money every month now. First of every month.*

That earlier rush of heat drained away, replaced by a now-familiar cold. *No,* she sent back.

How about I start coming by the house? Maybe I should get to know my darling daughter.

Her stomach lurched. *No. Let me think about it.*

The little dots didn't flash beneath her text for long before his response popped up: *Until the first of the month, sure. Drop me 5k then, and I won't say a word.*

With trembling hands, Holly closed the texting app and shoved the phone back in her pocket. What was she going to do? She did well enough with her freelancing, but she couldn't send Dylan five thousand dollars a month. Was he crazy? Though she didn't want to do it, it would be better to use the money to hire a lawyer.

Enough was enough. His threats terrified her, but there was no way a judge would give him custody, especially not after seeing all the texts he'd sent demanding money. She couldn't let him bully her anymore.

"That smells good," Violet called out as she sat her headphones on top of her tablet.

Shoving all her fear and worry to the corner of her mind, Holly forced a smile to her lips before she turned to her daughter. "Thank you, love. Want to play a game while we wait?"

"Yes!" Violet darted over to the bookshelf and grabbed her favorite board game, the cardboard box so worn that she had to hold one hand over the end to keep the pieces from falling out. "I think the tape on the corners tore again."

On her way to the table, Holly took a roll of tape from the organizer at the end of the counter. "I'll fix it."

And she would—she would fix the box and everything else.

CHAPTER 6

Chalmys did a quick check to ensure he had all of his tools before pulling the pile of gold coins close. He had more than enough of these after centuries of serving the royal family as a mage. They might as well be used for something. Even before his exile, he'd earned everything he could possibly need, most as rewards for helping defeat invaders or reclaim usurped peerages. Living alone, most of his needs met as part of his confinement, provided no cause for spending gold.

He'd watched human goldsmiths centuries ago, when most work was done by hand rather than machine, but his tools weren't precisely the same. Fortunately, he didn't need to employ the same primitive methods. Why use fire to soften the gold when he could use magic, instead? The important part was consistency. The magic had to remain uniform, and the pressure he applied had to stay even.

Technically, he could have used spells to replicate any design he wished; however, the result was limited by the scope of his mental vision. As a result, such pieces never turned out as well as something handmade. They might be fine from a distance, but any close inspection revealed the lack of fine details. It was no matter, though. He enjoyed creating beautiful things.

After lining the coins up across the smooth stone of his workbench, Chalmys grabbed a V-shaped clip from a tray along the side. He settled it across the bridge of his nose, then ran his finger over the tiny, inlaid stone at the tip. The magic activated, magnifying lenses forming as the magic sealed the device gently to his skin. It had taken years to perfect this little invention, but once he settled into the more detailed work, those years of effort would prove their worth. For now, he adjusted the magnification to its lowest setting with a quick flex of magic.

Chalmys tapped the stones hovering above the three other sides of the table, sending each crystal spinning one after the other. The magic stored within flooded over the worktable, and he gathered some of the energy into his palm as he locked the proper spell in his mind. Then channeling the power through himself, he brushed his finger across the line of coins as he loosed the spell.

Light flared bright against the gold, but it softened and began to meld at his direction. The image of his great-grandmother bubbled and then smoothed away. Quickly, he ran his finger back and forth over the metal once more, shaping it with his magic, until he had a single, solid piece glimmering atop his worktable like an elongated gold bar.

Though he didn't use fire, the metal could still grow uncomfortably hot during shaping, so he used pliers to grab each end as he stretched the bar into a long, thick wire. Then he snipped the wire into pieces with a clipping tool and set all but one of the chunks aside. He might not end up using them all, but gold, at least, didn't degrade.

Pliers in hand, he fell into the rhythm of pulling and twisting the metal for the first piece, magic pouring steadily from his hands to ensure the thinning wire remained the same diameter. He would need a great deal of this wire for the creations he had in mind, but it was a soothing process. Soften, stretch, shape in a constant refrain.

He had ideas for a filigreed brooch studded with pearls and a bracelet adorned with a line of semi-precious stones. But first, he intended to create a variety of simpler braided chains. These were fairly ubiquitous for any time period. As such, they should be easily sellable if he paid attention to the finer details. Like clasps. While scrying the shop, he'd spent at least an hour examining those.

And if Holly decided these were insufficient after all his work? Well, at least he found the task interesting. Challenges were few these days, so if nothing else, it was a pleasant way to pass the endless time.

The low hum of the air conditioner filled the otherwise-silent room, punctuated by the occasional click of a key or scroll of the mouse wheel. Violet was at school, but instead of working, Holly was immersed in research. The boring kind. She didn't care that much about jewelry, but she needed to understand it a little before she could sell it.

If she could.

Why had she said antique jewelry? Apparently, that was rarer—over a hundred years old, in fact. Vintage was the term she'd needed, since it would be more easily sold without any questions asked. But that presented new problems. Anything new enough to be vintage would fall under laws requiring a stamp that showed the purity of the gold. An ancient fae mage from another world wouldn't know anything about regulations like that. She hadn't, and she was from here. Unless he contacted her in another dream, she had no way to tell him, either.

And if they found a way around that? Then she had to pick where to sell the stuff. There was a sizable shop in the next town over that had a good reputation for fair deals. Of course, she had to offer something that would *be* a fair deal, not some scammy piece that couldn't be resold. Maybe gold buyers? The ads for some of those seemed shady, but they were apparently legitimate businesses. It was something to keep in mind.

Sighing, Holly moved on to her next, even-less-pleasant search topic. Custody law and family lawyers. She'd listed Dylan on the birth certificate, but she'd been assured at the time that it wouldn't automatically give him rights. That didn't mean he couldn't sue for them, though. Unfortunately, he could make life miserable with the threat of that alone.

But would he? That was the gamble, one she was going to have to take. If he was constantly asking her for funds, would he really spend what money he'd gained on a lawyer? Not to mention that if he did, she could start demanding child support. Right now, she didn't hold him accountable for anything. Was his current need for money really strong enough to risk that?

When her phone rang, she jumped in her seat, accidentally minimizing the browser window in the process. *Did I summon the bastard?* With a pit of dread in her stomach, she lifted her phone from the desk and read the screen. *Max-imum Annoyance* flashed along the top, making her grin.

Quickly, she answered. "Hey! Taking time away from grading papers just to talk to me? I'm honored."

Her brother laughed. "Exams are over, and I'm not teaching again until June. Which means I have plenty of time to pester you. Unlike Gavin, who called me early this morning on his way into work. Are you okay? He said you haven't been answering his calls."

Though he couldn't see her, she still rolled her eyes. She was the overprotected center of their family's sibling sandwich, with Max three years older than her at twenty-nine and Gavin two years younger at twenty-four. Both thought they knew what was best for her, but for different reasons. Max wanted her to get a steadier job. Gavin thought she should homeschool Violet and travel around the country, since she could freelance anywhere.

The constant suggestions were annoying, but she loved the interfering brats, regardless.

"He called *twice* in the last week," Holly grumbled. "Once at nearly midnight, and then last evening when I was putting Violet to bed. If he's going to pick such inconvenient times, he might as well text."

Max snorted. "On *his* phone? He wouldn't have the patience."

"True." She smiled at the reminder of their brother's old-style phone with the letters assigned to the number keys. But as a geologist, he was often out in rough terrain, so it made sense that he didn't want to spend money on a smartphone. "Anyway, it's just been...busy. Lots going on."

"Dylan," Max said, his tone going flat and hard.

She nearly groaned. How did he always know? "He's just wanting money again."

"So soon?" her brother asked. "His requests are getting more frequent than usual. Something's off about that, Hollyberry."

Not the nickname.

This time, she did groan. He only called her that when he was heading into Serious Older Brother territory. "Do *not* tell Mom and Dad. They'll insist on flying back, and it took them forever to save enough for this trip."

"You should probably be more worried about all *my* free time," Max countered. The clack of plastic-on-wood filled the silence. Great. He was agitated enough to fidget with the stuff on his desk. Probably tapping an ink pen. "Depending on what the bastard's done now, I'm more than happy to take the first flight over."

"No!" She grabbed the computer mouse and brought the browser window up. "I'm staring at the search results for 'family law attorney' right now. As soon as I find the best option, I'll make an appointment. I promise."

"Fine." *Tap-tap-tap.* "You still have the baseball bat, right?"

Holly laughed, but not for any reason she'd share with her brother. If she mentioned dream mages and bags of gold, Max would have a flight booked before the call was disconnected.

"Leaning against the desk right by my feet. Seriously, I'm fine. But if that changes, you'll be the first to know."

Her brother's sigh hissed against the receiver. "I'd better be. But call Gavin later, okay?"

Though she agreed easily enough, she suspected they'd play phone tag for a while. Gavin was three time zones behind her and probably hanging over the edge of some cliff looking at the striations in the rock. And he would work late, too, with so much summer sun.

As soon as she managed to disconnect with Max, Holly slumped a little in her seat. Days like today, she felt like an underachiever. Her older brother? The newest associate professor of his college's anthropological linguistics program. Her younger brother? Finishing a year's internship in his field while waiting for the first semester of his top-choice PhD program to start.

Her, on the other hand? She'd barely managed to get her Bachelor's, and that was mostly thanks to her parents. When she'd gotten pregnant half-way through, either her Mom or Dad had watched Violet so she could go to class. Of course, finishing at all was a major accomplishment. She knew that. But when compared to her brothers' successes...

Not that she would make the mistake of saying that around Max or Gavin again. They wouldn't let anyone look down on their sister—including their sister.

Well, there was nothing to be done about the past, but she did have an ex to cut off in the present. So she slid a notepad over, grabbed a pen, and started taking notes on the attorneys she was considering. If she did this a little each day between her other work, she might be able to have at least one consultation scheduled before the first day of June rolled around.

No matter what, she wasn't giving another cent to that bastard.

CHAPTER 7

$\mathcal{A}$ nice, cool breeze ruffled Holly's hair, though the intensity of the mid-morning sun suggested that the afternoon might tip toward hot. Fortunately, Violet would be tired of the park long before then. Or, rather, her body would be tired. If she had the energy for it, Violet would spend the entire weekend squealing through tube slides and swinging across monkey bars. Then an extra day on the swings for good measure. In fact, she would probably be asking for a push on one of those swings before long.

At the insistent chiming of her ringtone, Holly stiffened—then bit back a curse. She shouldn't have to worry about who was calling, especially not because of some loser who spent his days plotting ways to extort money from the mother of the child he'd abandoned. So she tugged her phone from her purse with a defiant jerk, only to laugh when she saw yet another brother's name on the screen.

"Sorry, Gavin," Holly said as soon as the phone was at her ear. "I meant to call you Thursday, but I got an emergency job."

A *hmmph* sounded over the line. "What kind of writing job qualifies as an emergency?"

Holly ground her teeth together. If people didn't stop being jerks about her work... "Well, picture a panicked HR rep who has to get an entire training manual over to her boss a week earlier than she'd originally been told. She's a regular client, in fact, so of course I edited it for her as quickly as I could."

"Still—"

"*Your* work has been waiting on you for thousands of years. Because *rocks*," Holly said sweetly. "Not that your job isn't important, of course. But maybe give me a break?"

"Okay, okay!" In her mind, she could see Gavin lifting his hands in surrender the way he always did when he knew she was right. "I guess I was being an asshole. But I had a reason for calling you, you know."

Out of habit, Holly tracked Violet's progress up to the top of the slide even as she processed the worry in her easygoing brother's tone. "Is something wrong?"

"I..." He sighed. "I had a bad dream. About you."

Her eyebrows pinched into a glare. "*That's* why you called at midnight?"

"Yeah, and you didn't even answer. What if I'd been in an accident?"

"The phone would have rung more than once," Holly countered, waving at Violet when she emerged at the base of the slide. "Anyway, tell me why you're so upset. I don't think I have long before your niece wants me to push her on the swing."

Gavin didn't answer right away, and his hesitation had a thread of uneasiness working through her annoyance. "It didn't feel like a regular dream, Hol," he finally said. "You were huddled against the kitchen counter with Violet, and that dick Dylan was standing in front of you with a knife. Then there was a flash of light, and you were just...gone. And Dylan ran out the back door, except the knife was in his stomach."

Whatever she'd expected, it hadn't been that.

"Holy shit," she whispered.

Suddenly, she had to fight back the bile forcing its way up her throat. What were the chances her younger brother had such a specific dream around the same time she'd experienced her own dream adventures? Could there be something darker going on with this Chalmys guy? But Gavin hadn't mentioned anyone else.

"And it was only me, Violet, and Dylan in the dream?" she asked.

"Umm, yeah," Gavin said, drawing the words out in confusion. "Is there anyone *else* who might want to kill you?"

Not that she knew, but that wasn't factoring in mysterious dream men. But then, there was no solid reason to assume her dreams were in any way related to her brother's. "Of course not." Probably. "I'm just confused. Why are you so bothered? You haven't told me about a nightmare since you were little."

"I have premonitions sometimes. Not usually dreams, but..."

Holly blinked. "You have premonitions? What?"

"Hunches, most of the time. Like where the rock might crumble beneath me or where to search for a specific mineral." Gavin groaned. "Look, I know it sounds crazy. But that dream...it felt like the time I got a flash of a cliff collapsing the day before it fell into the sea. Maybe I'm just worried about you. I don't know. But I want you to be careful."

Normally, she would have laughed it off, but after all she'd experienced lately, she couldn't summon even a hint of amusement. Here she'd been, considering whether a dream mage from another realm was actually contacting her, all while fielding increasing demands from her ex. How could she judge? And considering how things had been going, what if Dylan did escalate to physical threats?

"I promise I'll be careful," Holly said. "School's almost out, too. If things get too tense, Violet and I can go visit Max for a week or two. Unless you want us to help you find rocks?"

Gavin's laughter didn't hold its usual lilt. "Not unless you have no other choice. I don't even want to think about Violet near a cliff."

"Hah." Holly grimaced. "Yeah, same."

By the time she said goodbye to her brother, fear had set up a permanent residence below her sternum. So much for a relaxed Saturday. Now, she was going to spend the day picturing a knife-wielding Dylan. *Thanks Gavin.* She wanted to dismiss his warning, but the more she thought about it, the more she recalled all the times her brother had been right about stuff like this over the years. Like, say, when he'd told her not to climb on a certain tree branch—the same one that had cracked beneath the neighbor kid later that evening. Kari had broken both of her legs in the fall.

Maybe their family had some kind of gift for magic?

If so, it hadn't done her much good so far. It certainly hadn't prevented all this crap from crashing down on her at once. What would she do if Dylan broke in and attacked them? That terrible image ran in a loop in her brain until she longed for a spell to erase it. But Holly smiled when Violet skipped over. It was swing time, and she wasn't going to let Dylan ruin it. Not in dream form or any other.

If he tried to hurt Violet, he would rue the day.

A SATISFYING ARRAY of gold jewelry stretched across the left side of Chalmys's workbench when he finally stopped for the day. He'd requested a week, but it hadn't even been three days before he'd made enough. How long had it been since he'd done this kind of work? He'd forgotten how utterly satisfying creation could be.

There was only one thing missing, and that would require another dream consultation with Holly. Namely, the mysterious markings. When he'd examined the jewelry in that shop, the gold had all been stamped with letters, numbers, or symbols. He'd thought he could figure out what they meant if he considered the matter for longer, but it was a puzzle he hadn't been able to solve.

Although there hadn't been a great deal of variance in the numbers and letters, they weren't always used together. And the symbols? They varied entirely—when they were there at all. These might be a maker's mark, but he couldn't be sure unless he asked. Any variable that might ruin the value had to be accounted for.

With that in mind, Chalmys abandoned his workbench for the table connected to Earth's ley line. It was late here, and since the day and night cycles of the two realms generally aligned, there was a good chance Holly might already be asleep. If so, he could slip into her dreams and see what she knew about the symbols.

He let himself relax into the crystal's spin, following the tug of the path he'd begun to establish. In moments, his consciousness hovered over Holly's house. It must have been later than he'd thought, for the quiet of deep night blanketed the neighborhood. No vehicles drove along the street, and most of the windows were dark, including Holly's.

Only a lone man ambled down the sidewalk several houses away. It was an odd time for a walk, but there was no urgency to the human's steps. Trouble sleeping, perhaps. Not that Chalmys could say much—he was up and working, himself. Still, he watched the man for a moment longer, only resuming his task when he was satisfied that there was no trouble afoot.

Holly's house was quiet, except for the hum of machinery that forever plagued the human world. Chalmys slid through the hallway, making note of the calm energy emanating through the child's door, and into the bedroom where Holly slept. But not well. Her blanket was on the floor, and the sheets tangled around her legs like the vines of a dark mage's garden. She kicked against their hold as though truly trapped.

What had upset her? Quickly, he slipped into her dream—but not deeply enough to be a participant. A good thing, too. Dream Holly stood in front of a faceless, sword-wielding man, her daughter sheltered behind her. Had Chalmys appeared abruptly, her brain would have interpreted him as an additional threat.

Instead, he began to weave a thread of calming energy into the panicked snarl of the dream. She wanted defense, so he helped her mind craft a weapon. She needed victory, so he showed her consciousness a possible way forward. There was a strength he'd sensed in her from the beginning, and that made the task easy. She didn't *require* his help. Not really. His assistance only hastened things, and that was for his convenience more than hers.

When her dream finally shifted, he was ready.

WHAT WAS THIS? The forest again? Hadn't she been dreaming something else?

Peace reigned around Holly, only the call of night insects and the swish of tree leaves reaching her ears. But vague images haunted her every step across the soft grass. A Dylan-shaped figure. The clash of sword striking sword. Blood. Fear. Victory. Had that been her previous dream? It was already fading, the details slipping away. But this place? It was so real.

The grass tickled her bare feet, and moonlight gleamed over the clearing. A sweet-smelling wind shushed through the trees and ruffled her hair. And—Holly looked down—it ruffled her *nightgown?* The same one she'd worn to bed. Was this truly the mage's dream forest, or had she slipped out of her house into another reality?

Fear froze her steps, and she stared down at the silvery grass sticking up between her toes. Had the environment felt so real during her last dream with Chalmys? She couldn't remember well enough to be sure. *How* could she be sure? God, it would be just her luck to sleepwalk into a fae portal.

When her gaze swept up, he was there, his expression lined with concern rather than threat. "Are you afraid of me?" he asked softly. "Or are you still caught up in your previous dream?"

"I..." She swallowed against the lump in her throat. "I'm not sure what is real anymore."

He frowned. "Why?"

"Last time, I was wearing pajamas I don't even own." Her fingers picked at the soft fabric of her nightgown. "But I went to sleep in this. Am I really here?"

Like a flash, humor replaced his worried expression, and her breath caught at the sparkle in his uncanny eyes. God, he was attractive. If this was a dream, did he make himself appear more handsome? Tonight, he wore a simple shirt and pants rather than a fancy robe, but the way the fabric hugged his form...

It had to be augmented by his imagination.

"I give my word that this is only a dream. However, if you do this often, you'll grow adept at appearing how you wish," Chalmys said, and for a moment, she thought he was confirming her thoughts. "You can change your clothing now if you want, but I didn't bother. I'm afraid you have me as I've been all day."

Her dream-heart gave an unexpected thump. "I see."

"I must confess that I helped you through your nightmare." He swept his hand out in a slight bow, and the ties holding his shirt closed loosened. She had to tear her eyes away from the vee of his chest revealed by the parted fabric. "I don't know who was attacking you, but I'm glad that you won."

That snapped her attention away from the delicious hollow of his throat. "Oh. I don't remember the dream well now, but I'm pretty sure it was my ex. Violet's father. He ran off when I got pregnant, but he shows up to ask for money sometimes. Now, he's threatening to take Violet if I don't pay him more."

Chalmys's frown returned. "If he left like that, he should have no rights. Not without a great deal of atonement. A decade in service to your family, perhaps. That he dares demand anything is obscene."

A decade in service? Someday, she would have to ask about fae custody laws—if this wasn't another dream. "I agree, but I still might have to go to court over it. Anyway, my brother had a dream that Dylan attacked me. Gavin is convinced it was a premonition."

"Tell me the details," Chalmys commanded abruptly, his voice ringing with the same kind of power that she'd heard in that first dream. The one where he'd taken on an evil mage. "If you share both parents with this brother, he may also have latent fae blood. You might be at risk."

Though she stood in a warm dream forest, Holly shivered. What was this about? She didn't have fae blood. But Chalmys looked too fierce to convince, so it seemed more expedient to simply answer his question. Maybe talking about her brother's dream would soothe her subconscious.

And so she told him every detail she could remember.

"I will think on this," Chalmys said after she finished. "In the meantime...do I have your permission to cast protective spells on your residence? Perhaps something that would alert you to an invasion, if nothing else."

"Ah..." Holly stared at him. It seemed hasty to agree to such a thing when she hadn't decided if this was actually a dream. Then again, what did she have to lose? "I guess so. As long as Violet won't be bothered by it."

Chalmys nodded. "She won't be. Since I am a captive, I am unable to do much, so these protections will be far from full strength. Yet even if they were, I would ensure your child was the safest and most comfortable of all."

Did he have a soft spot for kids? He always wore the strangest expression when he mentioned anything to do with Violet. He looked defensive, for sure, and generally affronted that Holly thought he might cause her daughter harm. But beneath that, she could swear there was a hint of longing.

Well, it would make sense, at least if he really *had* been stuck alone in some fae realm for centuries. He wouldn't have had much of a chance at a family in a situation like that. An unexpected sense of shame drew her shoulders down. The man was lonely, and she was giving him a hard time about helping him escape. Though she did deserve payment, she didn't have to be rude about it.

"Did you pull me into this dream for a reason?" Holly asked. Then winced at her unintentionally sharp tone. "That...sounded rude. I mean, did you have a problem with the jewelry or something?"

If he was offended, he didn't mention it. "Only with the strange markings," he replied. "Do you know the meaning behind the numbers and letters imprinted on the pieces I observed?"

Just as she'd feared—he had no clue about the stamps jewelers used. Unfortunately, she didn't know a great deal, either. "I'll have to look it up."

He considered that for a moment, his finger tapping at his chin. After a moment, his eyes lit up. "I have an idea. If you leave notes on the matter atop your desk, I can scry for them tomorrow."

It was a solid plan, but Holly couldn't help but laugh. Now, even her dreams were giving her assignments.

CHAPTER 8

Thankfully, centuries of experience had allowed Chalmys to bury his seething anger beneath a layer of cool calm, for doing otherwise would have disrupted the dream and upset Holly. But he couldn't forget the fear emanating from her as she'd recounted her brother's possible premonition. It had shaken him deeply. So as soon as he pulled his consciousness back to hover over her house once more, he allowed the fury to burn through him before he lost all control.

He had no way to determine if her brother had the gift of Sight, but one detail stood out clearly—she'd disappeared in a flash. Not only that, but her attacker had ended up stabbed. Provided the dream *was* a vision, Chalmys could think of one possible reason for that. *His* interference. If he were to observe Holly under attack, he would certainly pull her to safety, and he would have no qualms about forcing some villain to stab himself.

But even if that dream hadn't been a vision, the fact that she was being threatened by some sorry excuse of a man made him want to rain lightning down on the Earth until the cur was struck down. Using a woman and then abandoning her, only to attempt to use her in a *different* way? And harming his own child in the process? Such a being didn't deserve to exist.

This Dylan was a fool, besides. Even on such short acquaintance, Chalmys could tell that Holly was clever, kind, and beautiful, and she protected her family with the strength of the fiercest warrior. To have the love of a partner like that, only to betray her? He couldn't comprehend it. Not to mention young Violet. Though Chalmys hadn't spoken to the little girl, the energy surrounding her was full of such sweetness and light that he had the uncomfortable feeling he would kill to keep her safe.

And *he* wasn't even her father.

That was what really riled him, wasn't it? The way this Dylan threw away the kind of family Chalmys longed to have... It struck painfully against the knots binding his lonely heart. Knots he'd tied himself, for otherwise, he wouldn't have been able to bear his terrible isolation.

Sometimes, life was intolerably unfair.

Oh, yes, he could see himself commanding that man to shove a knife into his own stomach. The idea brought a sense of satisfaction to his soul, and it was that which eased the force of his fury until it became more tolerable. He had to keep his emotions in check. With his vast power, it was paramount. He couldn't let regret over his own lack of family affect him so strongly, or others might suffer for it.

He wrested back full control with the force of his will.

His anger now a slow burn, Chalmys studied the area around Holly's house with more focused intent. Quiet darkness held sway, though the person from earlier was still out walking. With the dream in mind, Chalmys examined the man again. He was going the opposite direction this time, and he didn't so much as look at Holly's side of the street. It was still suspicious, no matter how casual the man appeared, but there was no evidence that he bore ill intent.

Why hadn't Chalmys thought to ask what this Dylan looked like? A lapse that would need to be remedied in his next dream with Holly. In the meantime, he turned his focus to the protections he would place on the house. The first thing he set up was an alert, one that would let him and Holly both know when someone approached the house. But in that, he embedded something additional: a special ping if that mystery walker crossed onto her property.

If he was simply an insomniac, that addition wouldn't be a problem for him because he wouldn't get close enough to trigger it. But if he was the man threatening Holly, he wouldn't be able to creep up on her house without causing an alert. Chalmys couldn't resist adding a little present, too—a slight shock that might make the stranger think twice about continuing. Really, the man was lucky. If Chalmys hadn't been bound by the gods and under observation, he would have cast more creatively debilitating spells.

Once he was as satisfied with his work as he was going to get under such constraints, he finally drew his consciousness back into himself. He blinked, and the crystal octahedron spun silently in front of his eyes once more. Suddenly weary, he rubbed at a tense muscle in his neck and sighed. How long had it been since he'd expended so much energy? Though it had once been customary, he must have slipped over time.

But this was a good exhaustion. He found himself eager to repeat the process on the morrow. Once he'd slept, he could break his fast and then scry to see if Holly had information ready about the jewelry markings. If so, he could complete that work and begin preparations for teleporting the new payment to her.

Thoughts of Holly followed him to his bed—and when he drifted to sleep, it was to the dream image of her lovely green eyes lighting with happiness at the gift.

WHEN VIOLET DANCED into the room with a chipper "It's wakey time, Mama," Holly groaned and pulled the covers over her head. It was always difficult to get up on a lazy Sunday morning, but it was doubly so after such horrible sleep. The only good thing was that her vivid dream with Chalmys had erased most of the nightmare about Dylan. All that remained were a few flashes of fear and clashing swords.

Like either she or Dylan would know what to do with a sword. Well, unless he'd taken up a new hobby after running off. Doubtful, though. Learning to sword fight took dedication and effort, and he wasn't particularly good at either of those things.

"Mama!"

It was her only warning, but Holly was prepared. When her giggling daughter leapt atop the coverlet, she wrapped her arms around Violet like a trap. Muffled laughter sounded from within the cocoon of fabric as Holly twisted, rising above her bundled daughter so she could tickle her exposed feet.

Violet pinwheeled her arms until her little head popped out of the top of the cover. "I thought you were asleep," she said with a mock huff. "No fair, Mama."

Holly shook her head solemnly. "I thought you knew all about the dangerous Blanket Trap, the fluffy cousin of the Venus Fly Trap. Very fearsome out in the wild, you know."

"Is not!" Violet cried, though she grinned.

Releasing a deep sigh, Holly shook her head. "Well, I suppose since you defeated such a dangerous beast first thing in the morning, I should make you a hearty feast in celebration."

"Oh, pancakes?" Her daughter shoved aside the coverlet. "Can I help?"

Holly hid a wince and nodded. It would take a lot longer, but she couldn't deny Violet the pleasure. "Go wash your hands, brush your teeth, and get dressed. Then meet me in the kitchen."

As soon as her daughter danced back out of the room, Holly sped through her own morning routine. It always took Violet forever, even with the promise of pancakes, so once Holly was dressed, she had a few precious moments at her computer to find that information for Chalmys. She was just spreading out the printed pages covered in jewelers' symbols across her desk when Violet appeared.

"Why are you doing that?" her daughter asked, frowning at the line of papers.

Well. It did look a little strange to have them all stretched out like that.

"I'll be researching this for a project later," Holly said, suppressing a pinch of guilt at the lie. "I'm laying them all out so I can compare the pictures."

Violet's eyes squinched close in concentration. "That's a lot of numbers and letters. Do some words have numbers in them?"

"No, sweetie." She ruffled her daughter's hair. "These are more like symbols than words. They tell you what kind of gold a piece of jewelry is. Since I don't know what they mean by memory, I thought I should have an easy way to look."

"Yeah," Violet said, her voice turning serious. "That's probably why Mrs. Wilkins keeps the alphabet on the wall. Some kids forget which one is little 'b' and which one is little 'd.' I just think of 'bed,' though."

Holly lifted a brow. "Bed?"

"Look," her daughter said, sketching on the desk with her finger as she spoke. "The 'b' is the head of the bed, the 'e' is the mattress, and the 'd' is the foot."

Holly smiled down at the fingerprint-smeared word now decorating the shiny wood of her desk. "That's clever."

"Mrs. Wilkins showed us. She knows everything." Quick as light, Violet's focus changed, and she tugged at Holly's sleeve. "Can we make pancakes now?"

"Sure." She eyed her daughter's hands. Had Violet remembered to wash them? "After we clean up at the sink. We don't want to get our food dirty, right?"

At her daughter's nod, Holly let herself be pulled toward the kitchen. Hopefully, she'd given Chalmys the information he needed, because the rest of the day was for her and Violet.

Monday would come soon enough.

CHALMYS HADN'T INTENDED to spy—in fact, he would have avoided that scene at all costs had he known what he'd be scrying into. Gods, what torture. It was a perfect morning where Holly lived, and the delicate light had shone through the windows to gild her and her daughter like the divine beings they seemed.

So sweet, that moment between mother and child. The love. The affection. The closeness. What would he give to share in a moment like that? To stand beside his wife and smile indulgently as their daughter showed them some new thing she'd learned? Would it ever be possible?

Even before being trapped, he'd struggled to find such a connection. So many feared his strength—or they coveted it. Either women thought he would influence their hearts with his magic, or they pretended affection in the hopes of gaining benefit from his power. Oh, not everyone, of course. But he'd grown weary of trying to determine who was genuine.

He might have tried harder had he known of the lonely years to come.

But there was no use pondering. He was stuck here now, and even if Holly helped to free him, his struggles wouldn't end. He would still be alone, and thrown into a different world, besides. Though his realm shifted more slowly than Earth, much had already changed the last time he'd scried. He would have to rebuild his place in society entirely.

Or go elsewhere—like Earth. He could create an entirely new life there, and if Holly... What? Came to care for him? Wanted to be with him? What was he thinking? It wasn't as though Holly could ever love *him*, a strange fae mage from another world, and young Violet would probably be terrified by the thought of a non-human. They would forever be their little family unit, and he would never—

Shock nearly sent his consciousness back into his body.

It would be foolish—absolutely foolish—to fall for Holly and her child. It was beyond imagining. He had to stamp all thoughts of that from his mind and heart. They were not from his world and never could be, and he had too much power to settle easily on Earth. If his thoughts kept drifting this way, he would have to seek another bard to help.

But even as he made note of the information she'd left for him, he knew he wouldn't.

CHAPTER 9

Holly tapped her finger against her desk with a frown. It was Tuesday morning. One week since Chalmys had promised to deliver the jewelry, which meant it should appear today. But it was already past lunch, and in a couple of hours, Violet would be home. Had he forgotten? Was it all a lie after all? Embarrassment seeped into her blood like a slow poison, but she couldn't take the leap to admitting she'd been wrong.

It couldn't have all been fake. Surely not. Maybe he couldn't do the spell if she was sitting here? The last pouch had appeared while she was out on a stroll. Holly glanced out the window and then groaned. Of course it was raining. She couldn't try that again, which was too bad. She could use a way to work off some of this restless energy.

What else could she do? Not work, apparently. Her concentration was crap today. But there was always housework to do, right? She rolled her chair back and was about to stand when her phone chirped with a text. The lump in her gut told her it wouldn't be good, and a quick look confirmed that her instinct was right. Dylan, naturally.

What have you decided? Do I get my money or the kid?

Holly shoved her fist against her stomach for a moment before she could bring herself to reply. *What is wrong with you?*

His response was quick: *Clock's ticking. One way or another, I'll get what I want.*

She dropped the phone onto her desk with a clatter. That was a threat. An actual, possibly physical threat. She didn't want to contemplate what he meant about getting what he wanted, because she was certain he didn't really *want* Violet. Not...for anything good. Oh, God. What should she do? The earliest legal consultation she'd managed to get was next Monday, and the following Tuesday was the last full day of school. She might have to wait until her parents returned from their trip next month to take any real legal action, since she wasn't sure who else she could trust to babysit during such a tense situation.

Dammit. What if Dylan really was planning to break in and attack her?

With Gavin's dream blaring in her mind, she nearly picked up her phone to call Max. He had free time, and she knew without a doubt that he would hop on the next plane if she needed him. But it was a terrible idea for one reason—if Max learned the extent of Dylan's threats, Max would end up in jail. He might be a professor, but he was a professor who could kick ass when he wanted to. Though her ex deserved the beating, her brother didn't deserve the consequences.

Who else could she call on? Gavin would cut his internship short to help her out, but that would threaten his reputation. If he decided to go into academia after he got his PhD, then...well, he might not get into academia at all if he earned a bad rep. She couldn't imagine that the world of Geology was a large one. She refused to mess up his future because of her asshole ex.

So...what? Hope the protections a dream mage had claimed to place around her house were real? She wouldn't risk Violet's safety for something that could turn out to be a flight of fancy. Even if his claim was true, Holly had no idea what he might have done or if it would work. She would be better off with her baseball bat.

Scowling, she picked up her phone. *I'll let you know on the first of June. Don't attempt to contact me before that.*

After a few choice curses, she stood. She wanted so badly to block his number, but then she would have no warning about his plans. She settled on leaving her phone on the desk so that she didn't have to see his stupid, dickish reply. Ugh. She definitely had to do something physical, even if she couldn't take a walk. The bathroom. She needed to clean the bathroom, didn't she? At least she could get rid of any *other* hidden, stuck-on shit she found.

ONCE AGAIN, Chalmys stood in the center of the stone circle and connected the middle crystal into the proper ley line. It had been easier to prepare for this part, since he'd already sent the coins through in the same manner. A fortunate thing, considering how long it had taken him to properly stamp his designs. He'd intended to send everything yesterday.

When Holly's desk clarified to his sight, he sent the new pouch through with a nudge of his magic. He couldn't hear anything this time, either, but he lingered a little longer than he had before. Had part of him hoped she would be there? Probably. Chalmys sighed at his own foolishness, but over the last couple of days, he'd given up on arguing with himself.

His fascination with her was simply inevitable.

Chalmys couldn't help but skim his gaze along her desk, curious to see if she'd left a note now that she knew he could scry. Alas, nothing. Her computer wasn't even on this time. Only... His gaze sharpened on the other computer—the small, rectangular kind that fit in pockets—as the screen brightened. Words appeared in a bubble that popped up across Violet's smiling face.

Make the right decision, bitch. I won't wait long.

Fury flashed so hot and quick that a lick of energy slipped through his hold, leaving a scorch mark on the stone at his feet—

and another on the wood of Holly's desk. Cursing, Chalmys hurried to close the link. Or mostly close. He needed to minimize the connection while he fought with his wayward emotions.

He took countless deep breaths before he was capable of grounding himself more thoroughly into the stone beneath his feet. Like lightning, the lash of his magic-charged feelings needed an outlet, and the bedrock circle made the perfect spot. But with a purpose. Gritting his teeth, he wrested back enough control to add the excess power to the spells imbued in the stone. Magic should never go to waste.

But even when he'd calmed down, he couldn't bring himself to close the connection without doing *something*. He had no way of knowing if he would truly save Holly the way he had in her brother's dream, but after seeing that message on her device, Chalmys felt certain that it was a distinct possibility. The threat in those words was undeniable.

Which meant he needed to prepare.

It wasn't easy to teleport someone into his shielded realm, and this time, he would need to bring two people. He could do so without planning, but it would take a massive amount of his energy. Not ideal. However, if he prepared a focus stone permanently connected to a spot in Holly's house, he would only need to activate it when needed. He could also create a twin stone to send to Holly to allow her to trigger the spell. A portable portal.

If the gods were observing him at the moment, then they were about to get a show, because he didn't care about any consequences while Holly was in such danger. Not that there *should* be consequences, since he was—strictly speaking—following the rules. He wasn't allowed to maintain a portal for his own use, but he wouldn't be the one using it, would he? And he was permitted to bring visitors for short spans. It had been long enough since he'd done so that he had every right to host Holly and Violet for a month or two.

Resolved, Chalmys dug into the pouch he always carried during such workings. What stones should he choose? Hmm. A flawless quartz octahedron for certain. Perhaps...iolite? And this one, a stone called moldavite that he'd obtained from Earth. Those three should suffice. Above the crystal already spinning in the center, he placed them in the energy stream, one floating atop another.

Iolite, Quartz, Moldavite—perfect.

With a thought, he set them to spinning before linking them. Then his attention returned to the sliver of the link to Holly's house that he'd left open. Carefully, he attached a new strand of energy to it. Once that was stable, he lifted his hand and caught the thread against his finger, weaving the magic into a new spell, a portal that he could open or close at will.

Then he took one end and connected it to the quartz rotating merrily between the other two gemstones. Light flashed as he drew upon the energy of the iolite and moldavite, weaving the power into that precious thread. The link solidified with an invisible but tangible snap, and at that sign, he tucked the entire spell into the quartz octahedron. He squinted against the glow until the power settled into the crystal, fully integrated.

The other two gemstones were gone, but it only proved that the casting had worked. Yes, the spell had gone well, indeed. Chalmys gathered the quartz into his palm and then smiled at its perfection. He had it—Holly's escape route. Now, all he had to do was create a linking stone to send to her.

NOT EVEN THIRTY solid minutes of rage-cleaning cooled Holly's ire. Instead, it had left her both angry and tired—but not at all relieved. And while action usually calmed her racing thoughts, they still circled in a dread-filled loop. Dammit. She needed to find a way to ease her stress. Violet would be home from school in an hour, and she didn't want her daughter to notice how worried she was.

Holly flopped into her computer chair and spun toward her

monitor—only to spot the large leather pouch a few inches away from her phone. Her heart gave a little leap and then began to pound. It seemed that leaving the room had done the trick. She reached out a surprisingly shaky hand toward the bag, but the sight of a black mark between it and her phone gave her pause.

Was Chalmys so sloppy with his magic? He hadn't been before. Yet as she traced the thin, scorched line, she had to concede that his skill might not be what she'd thought. Well, at least it was shallow. If she sanded the wood, the worst of it would disappear. But maybe she should leave it. Hadn't she wanted a sign that she wasn't going crazy?

Shrugging, Holly grabbed the pouch and opened it. She peeked in, but as before, it was difficult to discern details. So she set the bag on its side and shook the contents gently onto the desk. Even in the dim light of an overcast day, the jewelry gleamed like treasure. Like a dragon's hoard or a pirate's loot.

Most of the pieces were simple chains—if one could call such exquisite craftsmanship "simple." Had he really created these himself? Surely not. Holly lifted one necklace to examine it more closely. Tiny gold filaments had been braided together, then twisted into a delicate spiral. Near the clasp, she found the stamp declaring the piece to be 24 karat gold beside a marking that looked like a crystal entwined in a vine.

Well, no one would know that maker's mark.

Holly set the chain aside and picked up another. Then another, until she'd studied each one. Most were similar, but none were replicas, either. It would be obvious that these weren't factory-created necklaces, even without the unique maker's mark. But that wasn't necessarily a bad thing. After all, there were plenty of modern artisans creating jewelry. These could easily pass for that sort of thing.

But there were a handful of other pieces she hadn't expected. All brooches. Did anyone wear those anymore? Holly lifted the first one and gasped at the beauty of it. If not, this might change a person's mind. Gold leaves and vines twined out in a loose spiral from a center knot of emeralds, and tiny rubies were studded here and there along the vines like little flowers. The stones couldn't be real, could they? This brooch alone might be worth a fortune, and she didn't have to study the others as closely to figure them to be the same.

Either the man's story was really long and involved, or he valued her time more than she did.

Holly snorted. Maybe it was a little of both. After all, he was centuries old, so his story would naturally be long. Possibly a little boring after his capture, but still long. And God knew she didn't always charge what she should, though she made a solid living after so many years at her job. She had a feeling that this jewelry would boost her savings significantly.

She tucked each piece back in the pouch with care and pulled the drawstring closed. But just when she was about to carry it to her safe, a tingle raced up her arms and down her spine. The fine hairs on her skin lifted as goosebumps seemed to prickle every inch of her flesh. She froze. What was this charge in the air? It reminded her of the time lightning had struck just across the field from where she'd been playing baseball with her brothers.

But instead of the flash and boom of a storm, the light in front of her wavered and then...morphed? Shifted? Holly blinked, and a small circle appeared between her face and the computer monitor. She caught the barest glimpse of trees. Then Chalmys's face. Then some kind of cylinder blocked her view before a soft pop made her close her eyes out of reflex.

A hollow sound like a wrapping paper tube being thwacked against a table—or a brother—startled her eyes open just as the tingle faded from her skin. The circle of light was gone, but now a scroll of rich, cream-colored paper held together by a ribbon rested beside the pouch on her desk. What in the world?

Hah. Guess that answers the question about whether I can be here when he does his magic.

With trembling fingers, she lifted the scroll and studied it. The green ribbon tied around the center was lovely, even sporting a tiny crystal attached to one end, and the parchment looked to be finely made. If there'd been a wax seal, it would have looked like a secret message sent by the hero of a historical movie. Unexpected delight filled her as she unrolled the thick paper and held it open like the hero's treasured maiden.

Unlike the little note he'd left in the first pouch of gold, the handwriting here was somehow bolder yet more even—almost as though he'd printed the message from a computer program. Maybe he'd written the message with magic rather than an actual pen? Holly smiled. Ah, the mage's equivalent of a word processing program.

Holly,

Please forgive the mark left upon your desk. I fear I was overcome by the message left by your former lover. Though I have delivered payment happily, I question whether you might need an escape more than I do. Please carry the crystal wrapped around this message with you at all times. If you find yourself in danger, speak my name against it, and I will help.

However, I would be pleased to host you and your daughter as temporary guests now if you would like to find a safe haven before your brother's dream becomes reality. Being pulled to another realm abruptly and under such terrible conditions might be terrifying for both you and young Violet, so it occurred to me that you might wish to come sooner. I am allowed the occasional companion or two, and they are not bound to remain here as I am.

Although I doubt you trust me enough to accept, I assure you that the invitation is open indefinitely.

-Chalmys

Holly let the paper roll back up with a snap. Go to his realm? Was he joking? What kind of mother would carry her young child to the home of a literal dream man, one who wasn't even human? That would be ridiculously irresponsible. Really, she knew next to nothing about the guy. She still wasn't one hundred percent sure that he was real.

But despite her instinctive dismissal, the idea stuck tenaciously in her head even after she'd returned from putting the jewelry in her safe. What was her subconscious trying to tell her? That it was better to think about this now? If Gavin *had* managed to have a psychic dream, then she really might end up fleeing to another realm, at least if that's what the flash of light meant. Would she accept passage to Chalmys's world in a dangerous situation like that?

Absolutely.

He was probably correct that it would be terrifying. Violet would no doubt bounce back quickly, being so bright and cheerful, but there were no guarantees. The unknown could be scary for anyone. So regardless of what Holly did concerning the invitation, it would be wise to talk to her daughter a little about magic, fae, and other universes. She might not be ready to hop on over to Chalmys's home now, but she could definitely get an idea of how Violet might feel.

Holly tied the ends of the green ribbon together, leaving the crystal to dangle on its tiny loop of gold. Then she dropped the ribbon over her head and tucked it beneath her shirt. He'd said to speak his name against it, which should be easy enough if she wore it like a necklace. If she stuck the whole thing in her pocket, it would only fall out when she pulled out her phone.

Speaking of. Holly lifted it, examining the case to check for damage from the mage's misdirected spell. What had he meant about being overcome by a message? Could he activate her phone while scrying? Because she had to admit that it would be a little creepy if he was searching through her messages without her knowledge.

Then she hit a button and saw the chat bubble that appeared on her lock screen. Suddenly, she had the urge to scorch something, too. *I won't wait long.* What did Dylan mean by that? Dammit. If she'd thought the previous text was a threat, then this definitely was. Something really must have changed to make the asshole so desperate.

She needed to get Violet out of here as soon as school was over. Just a week. One week until the two of them could leave on a little vacation.

CHAPTER 10

*H*olly tossed the last handful of wet socks into the dryer and then closed the door. She hit the correct settings on autopilot. When should she talk to Violet? Bedtime stories might be a good place to start, except she'd probably have to head to the library if she couldn't find the right book here. Her daughter loved unicorns, fairies, and mermaids as much as the next Kindergartener, but Holly couldn't remember how the books about them portrayed mages.

It already bothered her how often witches were depicted as evil, even though there was an entire religion of perfectly innocent people who labeled themselves such. Like her cousin Mandy, a vegan who wouldn't kill an insect even if it was biting her. So yeah, none of those books were on Violet's shelf. What about wizards, though? And fae?

Classic fairy tales were definitely out—she couldn't recall a single good fae in any of those. Ugh. If it wouldn't cause more trouble than good, she would call Max for advice, since myths and legends were his specialty. But he would want to know why, and then she would have to come up with a reason that made sense.

Could she make up a story? That might be most effective in the long run.

"Mama!" Violet cried as she ran into the laundry room. "Why are you staring at the dryer? I want you to read me this weird story."

Weird story? Blinking, Holly spun to face her daughter, but alarm froze her mid-pivot. The scroll! How was Violet holding the scroll? She'd put it in the safe with the jewelry before the school bus...

No. No, she hadn't.

Palm pressed against her temple, Holly searched her daughter's face for signs of alarm, but she found only curiosity. "How do you know it's a story? Did you open it?"

"I didn't! You said not to read stuff on your desk cause it might be business, but only a magic story would be in something like this, right?" Violet lifted the scroll with reverence-filled eyes. "I have to know what it says, Mama. I *have* to."

Holly nearly groaned at the sweet pleading in her daughter's voice. How could she tell her it was an invitation given because her father was threatening to harm them? It would break Violet's tender little heart. Maybe Holly could...alter it a little? She didn't like to lie to her daughter, but sometimes, lying was for a good cause.

"Here," Holly said, holding out her hand until her daughter slapped the paper eagerly into her palm. "But don't get too excited. This isn't a story, but it is really special. Magic, even."

"Magic," Violet breathed.

Holding back a smile, Holly unrolled the scroll and made a show of studying it. "Would you believe that I, your average, everyday mom, was hired by a wizard?"

That brought a frown to her daughter's face. "Hired? That sounds boring."

"I guess it would be. Except wizard," Holly said with a chuckle. "I wasn't sure I should tell you, though."

The frown deepened. "Why?"

"Well, it sounds a little unreal, doesn't it? And maybe scary. Magic is a powerful thing, so I thought you might be frightened to learn that it's real." Holly pursed her lips. "*And* it has to stay just between us. It's a top-secret assignment."

"Oh." Excitement spread across Violet's face once more. "Oh, I can do that! But I don't think it's scary, Mama. Can I meet the wizard? What's his name? Does he have a unicorn? A fairy? What if he is a fairy? Have you met him? You have to look for wings. Except they could be hidden, so you'd have to ask nicely to see them."

Holly's lips twitched. "I've only seen him in dreams, but he didn't have wings then. I think he's fae, which is like...something between a human and a fairy, I guess. Oh, and his name is Chalmys."

"What about the unicorn?" Violet persisted. "And you didn't say if I can meet him. Can I? Please?"

"May I," Holly corrected automatically, though it wasn't a grammar rule she cared that much about. Or maybe she just wanted to avoid answering. If Gavin turned out to be psychic, there was a fair chance her daughter *would* meet Chalmys, but it was best not to introduce too much information at once. "I'm not sure if you'll meet him. You usually wouldn't, unless my client was local, and he's far from that. I'll ask him about the unicorn, though."

As Holly closed the scroll, Violet gripped her sleeve. "Mama. If he has a unicorn, I have to ride it. My life would be complete."

Holly blinked down at her daughter. "Your *life?* That sounds like a grown-up thing to say."

"I got it from Mrs. Wilkins," Violet said, nodding. "She said as soon as she gets to the beach, her life will be complete. I'm not sure it's true, though. Her life was supposed to be complete if her wish list got filled, but it did when I brought in pencils, and now she needs a beach. But I'm pretty sure a unicorn would do it."

Poor Mrs. Wilkins. Holly grinned. "Even for your teacher, I bet. Though I sort of hope Chalmys doesn't have a unicorn. It would be tough to have a complete life at age five."

She expected a cry of protest, but Violet surprised her by

giving it some thought. Ah, her daughter was so adorable when she tapped her finger against her little chin! "Is it one of those fig... figgy...figure... I don't remember the word, Mama. The thing when what you say isn't real."

It only took a moment for Holly to puzzle it out. With a writer mother and literature professor uncle, Violet heard a lot of technical terms. "Figures of speech? Yep. It's one of those sayings that's really an exaggeration."

"I should have known," her daughter whispered almost solemnly. Then she shrugged. "Well, at least I'll see Mrs. Wilkins next year. I thought she might die. Anyway, I'm going to go look for a unicorn book. I better research."

Just like that, Violet pranced out of the room—probably pretending to be a unicorn. Holly slumped against the dryer and let its warmth soothe her for a moment. Were children more like sponges or fire hoses? On days like today, it was apparently both.

The sound of her sigh was lost beneath the soft, repetitive thumping of the drying clothes. Well, if nothing else, at least she didn't have to worry about Violet being scared of magic. With everything currently going wrong, Holly would take it.

CHALMYS KNEW she wouldn't accept, not without true duress, and even the likelihood of that seemed slim. Not that he wanted Holly to be in danger, of course. But he felt a thousand kinds of foolish preparing his home for guests based only on the dream of a man he'd never met. Why go to so much effort when he didn't need to?

Rubbing the back of his neck, Chalmys stood at the door of his nicest guest chamber and cataloged its condition. Because apparently, he was a fool. Time and again, he allowed hope to outweigh caution. Yet what did he have left? If he didn't reach for some piece of that light, he would fall forever into the deepest realms of darkness.

So. What needed changing here? The desk, chair, and small dining set would be old-fashioned by her standards, but they would suffice after a quick clean. However, not being certain how many decades had passed since his last guest, he suspected the mattress and bed coverings would need his most stringent revitalization spell, if not complete replacement.

It wasn't as though he had anything better to do at the moment.

Shrugging, Chalmys held both hands outward and sent his magic forth. Little tendrils swept over everything—ceiling, walls, floor, furniture—and swirled every bit of dust and dirt into a ball in the center of the room. With a flick of his finger, he opened the window and sent the grimy bundle out into the garden where it could rejoin the elements.

That done, he directed the tendrils over and into every bit of fabric in the room. It wasn't in terrible shape, for the most part. He used the proper spell to return everything to its original state, even the mattress, though it required more magic than he preferred. But considering he still needed to prepare the bathing chamber and then the adjoining room for young Violet, it seemed prudent not to spend so much effort finding a replacement.

Fortunately, the bathing chamber was in good repair, needing only a solid sweep of cleaning magic to return it to normal condition. In only a few minutes, he was opening the door linking Holly's room to Violet's. He cleaned and renewed once again, but when everything was in order, he hesitated before leaving.

Would this room be suitable for a child? It was essentially the twin to Holly's chamber, the adjoining rooms designed for close travel companions or even noble spouses who preferred not to sleep together. Hardly a nursery. *Hmm.* The desk and dining table should pose no hazard, though he should probably check with Holly about the sharp corners. But the bed... The elaborately carved frame might delight a child, but its height might pose a problem. If the little girl rolled off the bed, she would surely break a bone.

No doubt, there were other considerations, too, and not just for Violet's safety. What else might someone from modern Earth require to be happy? Their computers seemed portable enough. But clothes? Toys? Hmm.

He definitely had a great deal more scrying to do.

It was Friday before Holly finally had time to make it around to the vintage jewelry shops in the area, and she didn't have long even then. She'd had two rush projects that she'd wanted to get done so she could attend Violet's end-of-school party this afternoon without having to stress. As it was, she'd barely sent the last one off before midnight last night, after which she'd promptly dropped into bed.

She didn't know what to think about Chalmys's absence from her dreams the last few nights, especially after his invitation. Was he busy? Giving her space? Maybe *she'd* been too tired to connect with? The constant wondering was enough to make a girl want to learn how to dream scry, but unfortunately, she had no way to contact him unless she did. She might have dismissed it all as a delusion if she wasn't carrying physical proof tucked into an old-looking jewelry box she'd scored at the thrift shop.

Time for more of that lying for a good cause.

The little bell jingled above the shop door as Holly strolled in, doing her best not to seem too eager or hurried. She'd brought one of the brooches and two gold chains, and a bit of internet research suggested they'd be worth quite a lot. Which meant she'd better not appear desperate. This shop had good reviews, but they would no doubt lowball the offer if they thought she had no choice but to take it.

To the right, a well-dressed lady smiled from behind an antique wooden counter. "May I help you?"

Like the elegant glass display cabinets arranged along the walls, the sales clerk's appearance and demeanor oozed genteel luxury. Nothing bold or brash, though. This was the ease of old wealth, the kind comfortable enough to allow imperfections to show—so long as they were the right types of imperfections. Namely, the ones you had to be rich to afford.

Such as old, expensive items with scuffs smoothed by time.

"I understand you evaluate antique and vintage jewelry," Holly answered politely. "Is that correct?"

Her careful words must have set the right tone. The lady's attitude shifted ever-so-slightly, her smile growing a hint more polite and her eyes revealing more interest. Smoothing the silken fabric of her button-down blouse, the clerk inclined her head like a queen granting a favor.

"Of course, Madam," the woman said. "My name is Eleanor, and I would be happy to take a look at anything you have."

Madam? Was this woman channeling a butler from Victorian England? Well, maybe she was. For all Holly knew, the clerk was really an Ella who drove a beat-up car and lived in the perfectly normal apartments on the other side of town. Actual rich people probably didn't ring customers up in antique stores, after all. If the posh attitude was an act, Holly wouldn't be the one to disrupt the play.

She set the box down gently on the counter. "I recently inherited quite a bit of jewelry and am considering selling a few of my least favorite pieces. They are rather unique, though. I couldn't say where they came from."

So far, all of that was technically true—using the loosest meaning of "inherit," anyway.

Eleanor took out a shallow, velvet-lined box and a jeweler's loupe from beneath the counter and then put on gloves. "Very well, then. Let's take a look."

Nodding, Holly settled the brooch and two chains into the box and waited. For the longest time, the clerk's soft gasp was the only sound that passed between them as Eleanor examined each piece. Then examined them again. She spent so long on the brooch that Holly nearly checked her watch.

When the sales clerk finally lowered the magnifying tool, it was with a look of awe. "I don't think I've ever seen anything like this. I've never seen this maker's mark, for one thing."

"I haven't, either," Holly said truthfully. "I couldn't find anything like it on the internet when I was doing research."

She really had looked to see if it was something Chalmys had copied during his research. As far as she'd been able to tell, the man had created his own little mark.

"And this brooch." Eleanor gestured toward it with the loupe. "The emeralds are extraordinary. The thing is, though…I'm afraid I'm too new to do an appraisal like this. I can give a rough estimate for well-known pieces, but it would be best to leave this for my boss. She's out for lunch right now. Would you like to wait until she returns? You could also leave the pieces here and come back for them later. We are fully insured, and I'll be careful to catalog each piece before taking it to our safe."

Although Holly was loath to let the jewelry out of her sight, time ultimately made the decision for her. She would never make it to Violet's party if she waited around for the appraisal. Fortunately, she'd already done enough research to know that this was a reputable shop. The jewelry would probably be safer here than in her modest little house and tiny fire safe.

"If you can check it in quickly, I'll leave it." Holly smiled. "I have an end-of school party to attend."

And really, she'd rather not go into an elementary classroom carrying a few thousand dollars' worth of gold. That kind of thing just begged for a disaster.

CHAPTER 11

*E*yeing the name written on the chalkboard-themed strip of paper along the top edge of the desk, Holly placed a cupcake on the little boy's plate. "Here you go, Noah."

He grinned up at her. "Thanks!"

"You're welcome."

The plastic package crinkled loudly as Holly lifted out cupcake after cupcake, moving down the row until the container was empty. Another parent had the other box, though, so Holly returned to the teacher's work table to pour drinks. Behind her, a video played on the teacher's computer screen, a larger version showing on the projector over the whiteboard. So close to the speakers, the music was obnoxiously loud, but she didn't complain.

Seeing fifteen Kindergartners wiggling along with the beat made up for a lot.

"Oh! Be sure not to pour any juice for Lily," Mrs. Wilkins said. "She's allergic to citrus, and there's orange in that blend."

Holly slid one of the cups out of the line so she wouldn't forget. Before she could ask what else to use, the teacher pulled a small bottle of pure apple juice from a cooler and filled the cup.

Then Mrs. Wilkins carried the drink to Lily without any kind of fuss. As far as Holly could tell, none of the other children noticed.

Pro level.

After the food was demolished, the teacher called the students to the carpet for a dance party while the parent helpers cleared the trash. Thankfully, it was a quick task with several people working, because Holly kept getting distracted by glimpses of Violet laughing and dancing with her classmates. How did her daughter live in the moment so very perfectly? Joy like that was hard to come by.

And Dylan chose to miss every second of it.

Nope. Not going to think about him.

Stubbornly, Holly took out her phone to take pictures like the other parents. These were the kinds of moments worth saving. She wanted to embed such perfection into her memories until it could never be pried free, not even with magic. *Hah. Looks like I'm thinking of a certain mage now.* Not that he would fit in at all.

Although...a sudden, clear image of Chalmys performing magic tricks for delighted children brought an unwanted warmth to her heart. She reminded herself rather firmly that she was only completing an assignment for him. That was absolutely all.

Provided he returned to her dreams, of course.

Holly was about to tap the shutter button on her phone when a text box popped across the screen, interrupting the view. Frowning, she lowered the device, but she froze as soon as she read the sender's name. Dylan. Of course he had to interrupt. The bastard.

I hope whatever you sold was worth a lot. Should I show up at the party for my payout?

Her stomach lurched, and suddenly, the sweet, cheerful scent of cupcakes and juice morphed into a nauseating mélange. *I didn't sell anything. Anyway, you said the first of the month.*

Maybe I need it sooner.

Just that. Holly waited to see if he made any other threats, but no more typing bubbles appeared. Finally, she shoved the phone back in her pocket, her hands shaking. He was watching her. How else would he have known that she'd gone to sell something? And he'd mentioned the party, so he'd somehow learned about that, too. Could he have made it onto the class email loop, or had he seen people carrying in party snacks and guessed correctly?

For the first time in her life, Holly truly understood what it meant to have her skin crawl. She had to fight the urge to rush over to the window or to peek out into the hallway for signs of Dylan. But aside from scaring the children, it would be pointless. The window looked out over the fenced-in playground, and visitors were strictly monitored. Anywhere he could find to spy would be too far away from her to see.

"Would you mind—" Mrs. Wilkin's words cut off, but her voice refocused Holly's attention. "Are you okay?"

Holly kept her own voice low. "Violet's father just texted threatening to show up at the party. But I didn't tell him about it."

Anger flashed in the teacher's eyes. "If you'll help hand out the presents, I'll quietly call the assistant principal. Don't you worry about a thing."

"Thank you," Holly said with a tremulous smile.

They both knew it was impossible not to worry.

As Mrs. Wilkins directed the children to return to their desks, Holly joined another parent in gathering up the small gift bags, each bearing a name tag. Thank goodness the students hadn't sat on the carpet—there was no way her frazzled brain would've recalled the few names she'd managed to learn. Even with the tags on each desk, it took longer than it should have.

She tried to delight in Violet's joy when she opened her gift— a book, stickers, and one of those pop toys, all unicorn-themed— but she was too hyperaware for that. Every chair scrape, paper crinkle, or squeal of happiness. Every shift of the light through the window. Everything caught her notice. And they still had to make it out of the building.

Holly tried very hard not to think about that.

CHALMYS HADN'T INTENDED to spy, but as he scried along the street in search of shops, he spotted Holly and Violet leaving their vehicle near one of the stores. Part of him hesitated to follow, just as he'd been reluctant to scry through their house for ideas. Now that he knew them, doing such a thing felt...intrusive. In fact, the thought of it made him squirm despite the intense concentration required to maintain the connection.

He shouldn't follow. He wasn't going to follow. But then he noted the stiff way Holly held herself and the way her eyes darted frantically around them as she took her daughter's hand. He drifted closer, close enough to see the fear carefully banked in her eyes. She was trying not to show it in front of Violet, but Holly was terrified.

That Dylan cur—it had to be because of him. Was she worried that he was nearby? Had there been more threats? A curse rumbled in the back of his mind at his lack of knowledge. He should have been more attentive to the situation. He'd let himself get so caught up in preparation that he hadn't really noted the passage of time, nor had he recalled how quickly things happened in the human world.

Or any world that wasn't locked away by a pernicious god.

He trailed behind them all the way to the door of a shop that proclaimed itself a seller of antique and vintage jewelry. That made sense. But the way Holly glanced up and down the sidewalk again...that didn't, not unless there was a threat. Why hadn't he asked her what her ex-lover looked like? It would have been easier to confirm whether the man was near.

As the two ladies entered, Chalmys lingered outside the door, searching the area for any hint of something off. Maybe he couldn't confirm if the man was stalking Holly, but he could make note of anyone acting suspicious. So he swept his awareness along the street, hovering above the heads of the passing humans.

The area wasn't terribly crowded, but modern human

villages were oddly designed, often in ways that lessened the number of people in any one place. In this case, the city did have a central square with a few roads branching away from it, but the stores here appeared older than the ones found around the outer edges. It almost reminded him of ley lines, the way the streets connected all the housing and shopping center nodes.

Here, there appeared to be two distinct types of people: those dressed in official-looking clothes who marched along the side-walk with resolve and those in casual dress who strolled by, pausing here and there to look through the shop windows. Both stood out clearly, for neither were exactly numerous. Yet both seemed to fit into the area. Chalmys circled the entire square without noting anyone acting oddly.

Then at the end of the row where Holly had parked, a flash caught attention. There. A man held his rectangular computer over the edge of the vehicle's open window. Chalmys slid closer. Based on what he knew of these vehicles, the man sat in a passenger's seat rather than behind the wheel used for steering. What could he be doing with the computer? Could it be used to scry— or even to attack?

Another man stomped out of a nearby restaurant. Balancing two paper cups, he slid into the master's seat of the conveyance. "Last time I'm buying you a coffee, Dylan. Your cheap ass needs to get a job."

Dylan.

Anger simmered in Chalmys's gut, but this time, he maintained control of his magic. Even when the bastard laughed and answered, "Why bother when my woman's on the job? She can pass a drug test. I can't."

"Funny how I've never met this girlfriend of yours." The other man shoved the cup at Dylan. "Take it. I have to get home before I lose *my* woman."

"Give me a few more minutes. I'm trying to get a good recording for Holly." Dylan's smile took on a wicked twist, though with his face turned away, his friend didn't see it. "She loves when I send her stuff. Helps with her research, you know."

So he *was* observing her with the little computer. Wretched device. Chalmys narrowed his focus on the computer in question. Was there a way to disrupt it? Even ruin it? These objects all hummed with a fascinating sort of power, almost like lightning contained. Perhaps he could leech that energy out—or add more to overwork it. Forcing too much energy into a crystal would crack it. This might very well work the same.

With that in mind, Chalmys carefully connected to the power streaming through the device. It only took a moment to adapt, since it *was* much like lightning. Once settled, he trickled magic through the connection, slowly at first so he could observe the reaction. It took surprisingly little before Dylan cursed and glared down at the little computer in surprise.

"Damn phone is getting hot. What the hell?"

A phone. That's the object's name.

His friend snickered. "Cause you buy cheap shit, man. Probably got one of those with the exploding batteries."

Pleasure purred through Chalmys's blood as he increased the trickle of magic another hair and watched the human squirm. Suddenly, smoke poured out of the side of the device, and Dylan tossed it out the window with a cry. Chalmys cut off the flow of magic, but still flames licked around the phone, its glass going dark and charred.

"Damn, shit, hell!" Dylan leapt from the vehicle and stomped on the thing to put out the fire. "I can't lose this phone. Fuck."

His friend shot an uneasy glance out the window. "You'd better. Look at all those people. Any minute, we're going to get cops."

Whatever a cop was, it appeared to terrify Dylan. He grabbed his coffee from the car, poured it on the phone, and then grabbed the still-steaming device with his thumb and forefinger to toss it into the floor of the vehicle. Then he practically dove into his seat and slammed the door behind him.

"Move it."

The engine roared to life, and Chalmys just caught the friend's parting words as he backed out into the road. "Your girlfriend better have enough money to get my car aired out."

With a strange sort of rumble, the car and its occupants were gone.

THIS TIME, Holly didn't stand at the counter with Eleanor. No, she'd been directed to a room in the back, where a tall lady in a smart business suit stood beside a desk to shake her hand. Margaret, she'd said. Holly had been nervous about such a fancy reception with Violet in tow, but the lady hadn't hesitated to direct her daughter to the chair next to Holly.

She'd excused herself for a moment to retrieve the jewelry from the safe, so Holly fixed her daughter with a stern look. "Be polite, and don't interrupt. You have your unicorn book to read if you get bored."

Violet fluttered the pages of the book with her finger. "Okay."

That resigned tone didn't bode well. Her daughter might be generally sweet, but she was still only five. And it had been a long, sugar-and-excitement-filled day. Anyone would be a little overdone at this point.

Margaret swept back in, placing a velvet-lined tray on the desk in front of Holly. "I'm sure you're curious about what these are worth, but I would love to know how serious you are about selling them."

Holly blinked at the odd statement. "Ah. Well, fairly serious, so long as I can get a good price. I'm not in a rush, though."

"I'll be honest, since my reputation is on the line." The appraiser leaned forward. "I don't think I could buy this brooch, not and resell it in a town this size. This is studded with thirty triple-A emeralds, and the metalwork is eighteen karat gold.

Considering the artistry, I could see it going for somewhere between fifty and a hundred thousand dollars."

Holly sucked in a breath, then almost choked on it. As she coughed into her hand, Violet gave her a worried look. "Is that bad, Mama?"

"No," she managed.

And yes. Hadn't she told Chalmys to make something simple?

Margaret smiled sympathetically. "Sometimes heirlooms catch us by surprise, huh? Since I couldn't identify the maker's mark, it's difficult to determine the age, but I would say this was created at least fifty years ago. It fits the style. I wonder if you couldn't make more from a collector hoping to solve the mystery of its origin."

"I, ah…" Holly scrambled to get her thoughts in order. "I think it was some kind of custom order? But I'm not sure."

"Well, if anyone offers less than thirty thousand, tell them to take a hike."

Holly frowned. "Didn't you say it's worth more?"

Margaret's shrug was as elegant as her suit. "Certainly, but if you're selling to a shop, they'll offer less since they'll need to make money, too. If I were you, I'd contemplate inquiring at one of the big auction houses. For the brooch, I mean. The chains are lovely but more modest."

What did that mean? After hearing the worth of the brooch, Holly was almost afraid to ask. She needed to know, though. "What is the value of the chains?"

"This one," the appraiser began, tapping her finger beside the thinnest of the two, "Would sell for between three and four thousand. Being larger, I could comfortably make four to five thousand on the second one. I'll give you a report with the estimated value and the reasoning behind it. However, I would like to offer you five thousand right now for the two chains. It's a firm offer, since I'm not sure how long it will take me to sell twenty-four karat gold here."

Holly stared down at the two chains. Beautiful—and apparently worth at least seven thousand dollars. Seven. How many more did she have like this at home? Eight? And that wasn't counting the other brooches, some more elaborate than the seemingly simple one she'd decided to bring. If this was what Chalmys considered average, what in the hell did the man's grandmother own?

Probably interpreting Holly's silence as doubt, Margaret leaned forward. "That may seem like a low offer, but I really do need to consider making a profit."

"Oh, no, I understand," Holly said. "I'm a freelance writer, so I know what it's like to run a business. I'll happily accept your offer. And the advice about the brooch, of course. It sounds like I should get a safe deposit box in the meantime."

"I would absolutely agree," the lady said, nodding.

Thirty minutes later, Holly tucked a small box containing the brooch and a check for five thousand dollars into her purse. She'd even left a business card, since apparently, Margaret was wanting help with the copy on her website and might be hiring someone for the job soon. Why not? Almost any lead on a job was a good one, after all.

"Alright, sweetie," Holly said to Violet as they pushed through the door. "One more stop, and then we'll pick up something from the drive-thru for dinner. Your choice. How about that?"

Violet tugged Holly's hand, pulling them to a halt on the stoop. "Mama, I'm tired. I don't want to."

There was an edge of a whine to her daughter's voice that foretold an unpleasant trip to the bank—especially if it took a long time to get a safe deposit box. But with Dylan out there desperate for money, Holly didn't want to risk holding onto a fifty-to-one-hundred-thousand-dollar brooch. In fact, the sooner she could get all of the jewelry out of her house, the better.

"I'm sorry, love. I have to get this done."

Violet's sigh could have launched a hundred sailboats.

Lips twitching, Holly turned to the right, her daughter trudging along unhappily beside her. Parking was a little tighter now, since there was a fire truck blocking part of the road, but the main branch of her bank was just on the other side of the square. Maybe if Violet was good, they could stop by the little local toy shop on the corner afterward. Might as well. She didn't see any sign of fire, but there was no telling how long it would take for the firefighters to finish whatever they were doing.

She did her best to ignore her uneasiness and enjoy the walk.

<h1 style="text-align:center">CHAPTER 12</h1>

$\mathcal{C}$halmys connected to Earth readily enough, but as he had earlier that day, he hesitated just outside Holly's house. Why did doing this disturb him so much now? He'd scried through countless human habitations and slipped into more dreams than he would ever be able to recall. Though it *had* bothered him a little at first, survival had won that battle centuries ago. He had no choice if he hoped to find the appropriate bard.

None then and none now.

So despite his discomfort, he slipped through the shields he'd placed around the house and moved toward Holly's bedroom. He stopped outside Violet's door, not to snoop but to study the flavor of the energy around her chamber. She and Holly hadn't seen the disturbance with Dylan, but if the child had sensed the fear surrounding her mother, it might be affecting her sleep. Thankfully, her energy remained calm, with a tinge of happiness and excitement. He hadn't followed the two of them once they'd left the shop, so he could only wonder at the source of the latter.

Once Chalmys entered Holly's room, he paused to scry the area around them. He tried to tell himself that he wanted to get a good view of her belongings for research purposes—apparently, she liked the color green—but he was well aware that wasn't the full truth. It was that guilt again. She was vulnerable, and he...he was intruding. For the first time in centuries, he had to force himself to enter a human's dreams.

Would he find another nightmare?

No, thank goodness. Right now, she was drifting, her mind in the pleasant space between dreams. This was optimal for him, for it allowed him to prepare the dreamscape at his leisure. Out of habit, he began to form the image of his garden, but then inspiration struck. The guest room. He could show her how it currently looked and get her input.

It was half-formed before he rethought that decision, too. Holly hadn't accepted his invitation, so she would no doubt find it presumptuous, if not outright insulting. Or creepy. Really, forming a *bedroom* in a woman's dreams? She would surely think the worst. What had he been thinking?

Naturally, Holly wandered through the dream-door before he had a chance to change anything. This time, she wore the outfit she'd had on at the shop, not pajamas, and there was awareness in the way she looked around her. She was getting better at this type of dream communication. A good thing—except that she would be less likely to accept any excuses about the location.

"Where are we, Chalmys?" she asked. Then her eyes narrowed. "Hah! Are you blushing? Can dream bodies even do that?"

Chalmys huffed out a breath. "I am well merged with my natural form, so you're seeing me as I currently am. I had simply... thought to change the location before you arrived. This one is not suitable."

"Really?" A smile broke across her face. "Because there's a bed? Worried I'll dream-ravish you?"

"You are in a surprisingly good mood tonight," he grumbled as his flush deepened.

What *was* wrong with him?

"Maybe." Holly shrugged. "I guess I'm just proud of myself for sensing you here and wandering over by myself. Oh, and it doesn't hurt that I'm five thousand dollars richer thanks to only two necklaces. Did you really design all of the pieces yourself?"

He inclined his head. "With my hands and my magic, yes. They are not replicas of something I saw on Earth."

"Incredible." Her gaze swept across the half-finished room. "This place looks like it would be equally beautiful if the dream image was complete. I'm assuming it's your house, right? I bet you designed it, too."

"I placed every stone myself," Chalmys admitted, though he didn't usually speak of such personal things. Powerful mages guarded the secrets of their domain too thoroughly for that. "I had thought to hear your opinion of the guest chamber, but then it occurred to me what impression that might give you. Forgive me. I would not wish for you to feel pressured into accepting my invitation to visit. I'll shift us back to the forest."

Rather than seeming annoyed at his words, Holly laughed. A bright, bold chuckle. Was this the same woman who'd been stifling her fear like an alchemist shoving a cork into the flask of an overflowing potion? What had she done with it all?

Chalmys stared at her in concern. "Are you unwell?"

"Because I'm amused?" she asked, her smile turning wry.

"Truly, your mood is not what I would expect."

Another shrug. "I'm sure I'll come to my senses when I wake. Don't worry about it."

As if he could obey *that* directive.

IF SHE WERE BEING HONEST, Holly would have to admit that her current happiness made no sense. She'd spent most of her waking hours after the party fighting her anxiety. Not even depositing her check or watching Violet pick out a unicorn plush had erased the creeping dread. Yet as soon as she'd entered this dream room, a sense of contentment had washed over her.

Safety, maybe. Could that be it? Did she actually feel *safe* with a stranger she'd only met in dreams? Her laughter faded as she stared at Chalmys's concerned face. This feeling...it was like the rush of pleasure after a thrill ride, that moment when your foot first touched solid ground. It was the wave of shaky relief after avoiding a car accident by only seconds.

All of her fears and concerns were waiting on the other side of that dream-door, but Chalmys banished them beyond that intangible gate. Not because of anything he did, precisely. Simply his presence held those worries at bay. The dauntless resolve that was an inseparable part of him. She had the sudden urge to slip closer to him so that she could pull in more of his strength.

A thought that kindled a new fear, one not so easily banished. Was she developing feelings for him?

Absolutely impossible. She couldn't think this way, not with this man. He was far above her in power, skills, looks—everything, really. Aside from that, no matter how beautiful this chamber promised to be, there was every likelihood that she wouldn't see it in person. Even if she did, she would still have to leave it. She didn't belong in an enchanted fae kingdom any more than he belonged in her average Earth town.

"There's the distress I expected," he murmured. "I'm truly sorry for my carelessness. I should have thought better of the room after your difficult day."

Her day? What did he know about that? Uneasy, she crossed her arms in front of her waist. Now, she had to fight the urge to step back. "Have you been watching me?"

"I was scrying some of the stores in your area when I saw you and Violet go into a shop," he replied. Was it her imagination, or were his eyes a little more shuttered? "I didn't follow you inside, though, or see where you went after that. However, your fear was palpable. I realized then that I've been remiss. I should have checked in with you more often to see if there have been more threats."

It was a perfectly reasonable response, and yet... Yes, he *was* evading her gaze. "You didn't fully answer my question."

A smile ghosted across his lips. "I suppose not. It's simply... with you, I have grown quite conscious of how comfortable I have become observing humans. It is shameful that desperation has removed so much of my courtesy over the centuries. However, I assure you that I've never been one to spy. My presence is only near in the moments before establishing a dream connection or when delivering payment."

Could she believe that? It was impossible to prove, since he could pretend he hadn't seen anything. Yet as she studied the red tinting his cheeks and the awkward way he shuffled on his feet, Holly found she couldn't doubt his words. Why would a hot, powerful fae man spend all his time staring at her, anyway? He could probably scry into the dressing rooms of the most beautiful women on Earth.

"Fine," she said. "But alert me when you're near. We need to work on some kind of system of communication in any case, since it seems I've accepted your commission."

His expression lightened. "Excellent. The sooner I can escape this prison, the sooner I can help rid you of your abuser with greater finality."

Wait, did he mean...? Her mouth dropped open. "You can't just kill someone!"

"The removal of one waste of life would not bother me, but in this case, that wasn't my intention." The deadly look in his eyes as he peered at her reminded her uncomfortably of his resolve when she'd been him during the memory-dream he'd first pulled her into. "Holly, I do not wish to distress you, but he was attempting to capture images of you with his phone when I scried the area around the shop."

Holly shivered at the mental image. And to think she'd believed her fear waited outside the dream-door. "I looked, but I didn't see him."

"He sat inside a conveyance...ah, a car, I believe it was called." Chalmys straightened his shoulders, almost as though he was proud. "I used magic to ruin his phone device. It seems that giving them extra energy causes them to burst into flames."

Oh, that was absolutely pride—and in an odd way, she shared it. Or perhaps it was simply awe. "You must have blown up the battery. I suppose that explains the fire truck blocking traffic. I didn't see Dylan on the scene, though."

Chalmys shrugged. "He fled with his scalded device. Perhaps the incident will distract him from bothering you for a while."

She should have been relieved, but a knot of worry wiggled up her throat. It likely would be a distraction for Dylan...for a few days. Then there was a fair chance he would show up at her home to pester her more incessantly for money, since he would have to replace his phone. What if his desperation increased to truly dangerous levels?

"I hope whatever protections you put around my property are effective," Holly said. "In case Dylan escalates things. If I can make it to Wednesday, I've booked a flight to go stay with my brother, Max, for a couple of weeks. It's not a long-term solution, but it's something."

Chalmys's lips turned down, and disappointment flashed in his eyes. Dammit. She should have considered her words more carefully. The mage was waiting for an answer to his invitation, and she'd announced that she was going somewhere else before giving him one. It was just...she hadn't fully decided herself. Every time she settled on delivering a firm no, something inside held her back.

"I appreciate your kindness..." she began.

"But traveling to my domain is risky," Chalmys finished. "I understand. Had I a child, I would be loath to risk her safety, too. However, please know that the invitation is always open, free of any obligations or expectations. Our other agreement is not connected, and my hospitality demands nothing of you."

Her brow furrowed in confusion at the strangely formal tone, but then she recalled the legends she'd heard about the fae. "Does that mean that eating your food won't trap me for a few hundred years?"

He chuckled. "Indeed, it does."

A hint of haziness muffled her thoughts, followed by a strange stirring. Was her brain shifting to a new phase of sleep, or was there an external disturbance? Holly examined the sensation for a moment before deciding on the former. Huh. She actually was getting better at this. Who would have expected?

"I think I need to go," she said. "Which sucks, because we didn't get to talk about your project. How about I write out my ideas and leave them on my desk for you to look at tomorrow? Just...signal me somehow when you're there, okay? Something that won't scare Violet. Ah, shit. Violet. She wanted me to ask if you have a unicorn."

"A...unicorn?" Chalmys's brow lifted. "It's been some time since I've tamed one of the vicious, stabby creatures, but last I checked, there was a small herd deep in the forest."

Vicious. That didn't sound like the darlings of modern children's fantasy, but Holly didn't have time to pursue the truth of the matter. "Great. If we do end up at your house, I hope you have a solid fence."

Because chasing her daughter through a mystical forest going after "stabby" unicorns was absolutely *not* something Holly needed to deal with.

AFTERNOON LIGHT GILDED the little suns and rainbows dancing across the coverlet in Chalmys's guest room, but he could find no happiness in the cheerful sight. Not when he needed to redo the design yet again. Three times, he'd attempted to create a pattern a child would find pleasant, only to discover last night that he'd omitted one crucial detail.

Unicorns.

He wouldn't have thought they would fit the theme, but after scrying a little more on Earth, he'd discovered a plethora of children's objects featuring some semblance of the creatures. Truly, the humans must have gotten confused somewhere in their history, for these depictions reminded him more of the fae-born Elicornae, sentient, winged beings who also had a single horn on their heads. Perhaps the humans had heard those stories from the same inept bards who'd attempted to interpret *his* tale.

Unfortunately, Chalmys didn't have friends among the Elicornae, and it wouldn't have mattered if he had. Holly and Violet would be his limit of visitors, so he couldn't have invited an Elicornai to visit, anyway. But taming a unicorn wouldn't help. The child would no doubt be disappointed by the rough, drab, shabby fur and frightened by the sharp horn. Even *he* was a little afraid of the things, for a unicorn's horn spanned nearly the length of his arm.

So. Images based on the Elicornae it was. After releasing a long breath, Chalmys set to work, using his magic to shift the suns and rainbows until he could fit the new element in. It wasn't taxing, really, but it was boring. He would far rather be crafting something completely from scratch than be changing its appearance alone. Perhaps if Holly's attempt at helping failed, he could use the subsequent decades to learn how to weave.

Once he was satisfied enough with the pattern, he blinked away the remnants of magic sparkling in his vision and glanced around the room. He hadn't changed a great deal beyond lowering the furniture, but he had added a chest at the foot of the bed containing a few dolls and toys—and as of this morning, a set of unicorn figurines. Though logic still told him it was all a waste of time, especially after last night's conversation with Holly, something inside him screamed that he needed to prepare.

Ah, well. Even if it was longing or foolish hope prompting him to do this, what did it matter? He had more unclaimed time than any sentient being ever should. What else did he have to do with his day while waiting to check for Holly's note? At this point, he almost *was* bored enough to go tame a unicorn.

He'd just started walking back to his workshop when a deep, resonant sound-feeling reverberated through him with undeniable demand. He cursed at the summons. Vier. His greatest enemy, and all the worse because he'd once been a friend. If Chalmys had ever believed the amiable God of Bardcraft would turn on him so, he never would have allowed such closeness.

Striding through his workshop, Chalmys pressed a crystal on the wall to unlock the room guarding the communication stone. As soon as he stepped through the door, his teeth clenched in reaction. He breathed in through his nose, hoping to ease the anger, but as always, maintaining control was a challenging thing. He detested coming in here. Once, the room had contained multiple stones and mirrors for speaking with friends across multiple dimensions.

Now, there was only the link to his captor.

Unlike the magical items in his workroom, Chalmys had never bothered to design a proper setting for the large, clear crystal. It sat in the same awkward position where Vier had carelessly tossed it after removing everything else. If the thing rolled off, then so be it. The traitor of a god could bring another one.

Chalmys tapped the crystal to activate the link. "What?" he snarled.

"Dearest friend, is that how you greet a god?" Vier asked, a laugh underpinning his voice.

"If I were dear to you, you wouldn't have cast me into torment." Chalmys scowled at his reflection in the smooth crystal. He had no clue if the god could see him, but it hardly mattered. He would deliver the same expression in person. "Why have you sought me out?"

"Upon sensing so much magic coming from your estate, I thought it prudent to investigate." Vier fell silent for a moment. "Why have you been duplicating children's items? There were even a few such objects on your latest request for goods."

Chalmys had to force his teeth to unclench. "I dislike the insinuation in your tone."

"I dislike the thought of you abducting children," the god countered flatly.

He thought...? Chalmys's nails bit into his palms. "I have found another Earth bard who is willing to assist me, but she has a child. I only prepare in the event they need to travel here as my guests. Which I am allowed."

Was that hiss a relieved sigh? "Take care. Stealing human children has been forbidden for a reason. The presence of one will certainly raise questions at the next council."

"There is no law against a mother bringing her child of her own free will," Chalmys snapped. "Or no few of you would be several offspring short."

Vier barked out a laugh. "A point well-made."

"Is that all?" Chalmys asked.

"For now. But know that I'll be on my guard."

The connection cut off before Chalmys could reply, but like his expression, it didn't matter. Vier had made his point all-too-clearly. If Chalmys acted too hastily concerning Holly or her wretch of an ex-lover, it could bring the god to his doorstep—or earn censure from the council of gods. He would have to ensure that any action was well worth it.

With that in mind, he didn't linger over Holly's note the way he wanted. He scried the area quickly, memorizing her words so he could write them down in his own realm. The directions were simple enough, in any case. For the next two days, he was to create a loose outline of major life events, and if possible, send a scroll of such through.

That would absolutely use enough energy to grab Vier's notice, but it would be an allowed part of Chalmys's punishment —probably. In truth, it had never occurred to him to send written details. He'd never connected strongly enough with previous bards for such open communication, and in the past, many of them had worked more readily with verbal tales, anyway.

But the trick would be mentioning his birth and childhood without including incriminating details about his mother. Most were aware that he'd grown up as an orphan at the temple, but if someone had to tell his true story, it would be difficult to leave it at that. Yes, his mother had claimed he was a child she'd found during her assignment at his father's estate. Yet that wasn't the bulk of the tale.

Like the fact that she'd "found" him immediately after giving birth to him.

Well, he would simply have to do his best. He needed to deliver what he could within two days' time, because Holly and her daughter would be journeying to her brother's home the day after that. She'd made note that he could contact her through dreams if he was able but that he could not send her items while she was there. Understandable, as it would be difficult to explain something appearing from thin air.

The last part of her note, however, was more difficult to comprehend. *Even incomplete, your guest room seemed nice enough. The only other thing I could hope for is a place to plug in a laptop, but that's a bit too much of an Earth thing. Not that I'll be visiting. I just thought you should know.*

Plug in a laptop. He had no idea what she meant, but he had a feeling it would be interesting to find out.

CHAPTER 13

$\mathcal{H}$olly slammed her car door shut and then dropped her head onto the steering wheel with a thump. She could have spent the last hour wrapping up her current project instead of wasting her time at the law office. Not that it was the attorney's fault—she'd been helpful enough. The state's custody laws, however, were shit. There really were no protections against an absentee father, not even if he sounded threatening.

She could file a restraining order, but it might not be granted without an actual, clear threat of violence. And she couldn't stop Dylan from suing for custody or visitation. Unless she could get him to sign a document waiving all parental rights, she would have to go to court to do much of anything. The question was simply who took it there first.

So she could call his bluff in the hopes that he wouldn't shell out the money for lawyers and court fees, or she could go ahead and take on the financial burden now, filing suit first. Either way, if she got the wrong judge, Dylan could end up with access to Violet. There was at least one in the area with a soft spot for fathers—which was honestly a good thing except in a situation like this.

Fabulous.

Before starting the car, Holly placed her phone on the center console, but as she swiped the screen in search of her music app, a message popped up. Her heart stuttered, then raced at the sight of the icon for the class communication app. *Mrs. Wilkins: The assistant principal thinks he saw that man again. I hope you'll be extra careful at the bus stop.*

Holly hadn't heard a word from Dylan since Friday, and it had been a long weekend of jumping at every sound. Now this. She glanced at the time on her phone before typing out her reply. *I'll pick her up as a car rider. I know tomorrow is a two-hour day, but I don't think Violet will attend. I want to head to the airport early.*

I understand, Mrs. Wilkins answered. *I'll walk Violet to your car myself. She's a sweet child, and it's been a pleasure to have her in my class.*

After sending a thank you, Holly started the car. The Bluetooth picked up her music, but the cheerful tune didn't quite satisfy. *I should have set it on the angry playlist,* she grumbled to herself. But she could only grip the steering wheel until her palms hurt. It was the end of Violet's first year of school, and instead of the standard goodbyes, her first teacher had to send Holly a heads-up about Dylan. Did he have to ruin *everything?*

She let herself snarl a few choice curses for a moment before backing out of her parking spot and heading toward the school. Along the way, she scanned the sidewalks as much as she could, but if her ex was hanging around the area, she caught no sight of him. Was the bastard some kind of spy? Had he joined the military between rounds of extortion?

Holly broke out laughing at the thought of Dylan actually *doing* something, earning her a curious glance as she pulled up next to another car in the pickup line. Oh, well. The lady would just have to think she was strange. There were some things in life that were too ridiculous to be ignored, and this whole situation happened to be one of them.

Too bad she hadn't realized what a loser Dylan was before

she'd started dating him. He'd been the fun student, the one who'd entertained the class with his ready smile and quick wit. Quite simply, he was the kind of All-American guy that everyone loved. Only a few of their classes had overlapped during her first year of college, but in almost every one, there'd been a group of girls dedicated to admiring him. One group had even dubbed him Prince Charming.

That should have been her first clue, really. Like the prince who'd ordered his servant to find his girlfriend with a shoe, Dylan had coasted by on other people's effort. She'd already been getting sick of how heavily he leaned on her for help with his assignments and had considered ending the relationship right before she accidentally got pregnant. After that, though, he'd sworn he would change.

Right until the end of the semester, when he'd quit school and all but disappeared.

But Holly wouldn't undo the past, not if it meant losing Violet. The only thing she might change was not getting Dylan to give up his parental rights before he realized he could use them to grift. He would have signed just about anything after he'd first found out.

She rested her head against the seat and closed her eyes, though she would only have a few moments. In five minutes, the bell would ring, and she would have to shove all her worries aside to be present for her daughter. Right now, Violet was excited about her flight to see Uncle Max, and Holly would rather keep it that way.

They only had to make it through the night.

"I'M NEVER GOING to make this deadline," Chalmys muttered aloud, though there was no one present to hear.

He ran his hand through his hair for the thousandth time and shuffled through the papers as though half his life would magically appear on the remaining blank pages. How could he only have the first few centuries outlined after two days? He hadn't included many details about his training or the various alliances and battles he'd participated in, yet he hadn't even reached the part of his life where he'd been cursed. How in the world would Holly manage to actually write it all out?

He needed to send her a few more bags of jewelry—and perhaps one to every bard or their descendants he'd worked with in the past. He flushed with shame at how he'd treated them. He'd been an arrogant fool to consider this a simple matter. No wonder they hadn't put much effort into getting the details right. He was ready to skip things out of desperation, and it was his life.

As darkness fell, he was finally forced to write a note at the end of what he had: *Hopefully, this will be enough for a solid beginning. I will continue with the rest while you are away at your brother's house. Please forgive me for the delay.*

Chalmys did his best to roll up the thick stack of parchment, but it was a far messier bundle he carried to the stone circle than the last one. Twice, the ribbon almost came undone. Grumbling, he summoned a second ribbon to his hand and secured both around the sloppy scroll with a temporary spell. He should have found a dowel to wrap the whole thing around, but it had been so long since he'd sent a missive like this that he hadn't considered it.

At the circle, he illuminated the lanterns situated atop the four tall stones that sat at the cardinal directions. Then he placed each necessary crystal in its slot and gathered more magic into himself. As soon as he'd activated the crystals, he slipped into the proper ley line with ease. He no longer had to really search for Holly—he'd scried the surrounding area too often for that. *Of course* he reached the perimeter of her home's shielding as quickly as he could blink. Practice and habit made for excellent channels to one's preferred destination.

He sent a small, tinkling chime through the shields, the promised signal of his arrival. He'd done the same when scrying for her note, but he hadn't been able to tell what she thought of his method. Even if he'd been able to stay for long, she'd appeared too shocked to say anything about it. This time, however, he detected a stirring of a response—the slightest hint of assent. Had she begun to notice and even use the shielding he'd left? A fascinating possibility, but he shouldn't have been surprised. She did have fae blood, after all.

Chalmys slipped quickly through the shields, into her main living area where she kept her desk. This time, she waited a couple of steps away, and she wasn't alone. Violet stood beside her with a perplexed look, no doubt a little concerned that her mother was staring at the empty space above her desk. He grinned. If was going to do enough magic to warrant Vier's notice, he might as well make a show of it for young Violet.

He opened his eyes, and his attention split between the two realms. With a wave of his hand and a flex of power, the octahedron's spin increased until it was a blur. A glowing oval formed above it, which he manipulated until he could solidify the link—then open it. The child gasped and then clapped as the portal flared to life with an ostentatious display of sparkles before settling into something more like glass.

Now, he could look at them with his own eyes, though the oval was smaller than he would have liked. Since sound wasn't part of this spell, he couldn't hear with his physical ears, but through his scrying, he caught Violet's excited exclamations. Naturally, her first question was to ask if he'd found a unicorn yet. He smiled across the link, though he had to shake his head no about owning one of the creatures.

"What about dragons?" she asked, a stream of dragon questions following before he could figure out how to answer.

Chalmys gave Holly a tentative mental nudge. She probably wouldn't know what it meant, but—

The connection opened.

He gaped at her for a moment before he recovered his composure. *"You are learning."*

"Can he talk, Mama?" Violet asked with concern. "Does he not know about dragons?"

"He's going to speak into my mind," Holly replied aloud. Then she shrugged at him. *I've read enough books to figure it out, at least this kind of thing. It's like the dream link.*

"In a way, yes."

When her daughter tugged at her shirt, Holly sighed. *What should I tell her about dragons?*

He flicked an instinctive glance toward the sky. *Tell her there are none in my realm, but I would be cautious to offend any if there were.*

After relaying his words, Holly placed her hand on her daughter's shoulder. "Sounds like they're fierce, huh? Now, I'm sure Mr. Chalmys is working hard to keep this spell going so he can send something through for me. He doesn't have time to answer all these questions."

"Oh." Violet bit her lip, then nodded. "Maybe if I write them down, you can send them to him, and then he can make another pretty oval to give me answers."

"Violet..."

He nodded before Holly could say more. *You may have her do so. I don't mind.*

Head tilting, she studied him for a moment, her expression unreadable, before smiling down at her daughter. "I think that would be okay, as long as you don't go overboard."

"Yeah, he probably has important wizard stuff to do," the little girl said. "I'm going to go get started, okay? Maybe I can finish before the plane."

As the child danced her way out of the room, it was impossible for Chalmys to hold back his smile. He hadn't been around any little ones for centuries, so he'd forgotten how refreshingly bright and honest they could be. Even fae children who grew up to be circumspect in adulthood were so, and it lightened the heart.

Holly lifted a brow in question, though a slight smile curved her lips, too. Before she could tease him for being soft to her daughter's questions, Chalmys lifted the scroll. *"This one is heavier and is at risk of unwinding. Could you catch it?"*

She hesitated briefly before closing the distance and holding her hand out beneath the little portal. He'd shoved the last scroll through without much thought, but this time, he extended his own hand with care. It was oddly sensual, the way she took the other end of the scroll while he still held the other side. A link between worlds, only a bit of parchment and a capricious god's curse separating their flesh.

Though the portal was small enough that he couldn't see her face while passing something through, he was loath to release that simple connection. Ah, but he could still scry, wavery though it was with his attention so caught in this moment. He caught the blurred image of her staring down at her hand before he finally released his hold.

Chalmys sucked in a ragged breath before daring to look through the portal with his own eyes once more. She held the scroll gently, her attention on keeping one of the ribbons from unwinding. The holding spell he'd used must have been too simple to survive the crossing—or he'd spent more time here than he'd intended.

"I must go," he whispered into her mind. *"I'll visit your dreams in a couple of days, once you've recovered from your travels. You'll have to pick a new spot to leave notes, including young Violet's questions."*

This time, there was a strange, almost tremulous tilt to her smile. *"Thank you. I'll look forward to it."*

He held her gaze for a few heartbeats more, but he couldn't remain like this for long. If he lingered, Vier would wonder about it. So he closed the portal spell and then drew his consciousness back through the ley line until he was fully integrated with himself once more. Staring at the still-spinning octahedron, he rubbed at the unusual pinch of pain in his chest.

He must have overextended himself to ache from magic use.

Suddenly tired, Chalmys slowed the crystal to a halt before plucking it from the air and summoning the other crystals to his hand. Then he turned to march back to his house and the sleep he so clearly needed. He'd done what he could to record much of his life, and with Holly about to travel, he could spare himself a solid rest. Surely, she wouldn't need more of the outline so soon.

And maybe if he had enough sleep, he wouldn't think of passing over a scroll as *sensual*.

What foolishness.

HOLLY ANCHORED the curling edges of the parchment against her desk with a little cat figurine on one end and a chunk of raw amethyst from Gavin on the other. The dark slashes of Chalmys's bold writing filled the first page, the sight making her breath hitch and her palms sweat like she'd just received a note from her middle school crush. How silly. This was work and nothing more.

Still, she couldn't resist running her finger over the indentations left by his pen. Or quill. What did a fae mage use? Perhaps she should ask—ah, damn, now she was turning into Violet with all her questions. Holly groaned. What did it matter how he wrote things down? There were a *lot* of papers here, and that meant she had plenty of work to do. She couldn't afford to go off on a tangent.

With that in mind, she started reading, though immediately she noticed a problem. He'd said almost nothing about his birth. Literally a year, a dash, and "birth." His childhood wasn't much better, mentioning only that he'd lived as an orphan at some temple for a certain span of years. Nothing about his parents or what his life had been like. Just the barest of information.

Holly skimmed down to where his training began, and the difference was stark. Here he gave months along with years, and though cursory, he mentioned teachers and fellow students by name. She moved the amethyst so she could turn the pages. Now, there were anecdotes of amusing pranks and interesting assignments. He even listed when he'd switched dormitories as a teen and then later moved to more private lodgings for the apprentices nearing adulthood.

Heat flushed through her at the mention of his first lover, also by name. Centuries had passed, yet he still remembered the woman's name. Well, at least he wasn't careless. But would such... events...repeat throughout his outline? Holly fanned herself with a piece of mail and hoped he would be skimpy on the details about that. Or maybe really, really talented at providing the details.

Bad, Holly. Bad, bad, bad.

Fanning harder, she read on, skipping around the entries to get an idea of their depth—and passing over mentions of lovers before her heart pounded out of her chest. From a few lines alone, it wasn't difficult to form a picture of him as a man. Much of it matched the first dream she'd had of him, where he'd confronted some wicked mage. Time and again, he'd stepped into danger.

Without a qualm, too. He didn't say so, but it was written in the matter-of-fact lines of dispassionate text. He considered it a duty, no more remarkable than going to an office job. If office jobs included leveling the stronghold of a fae demigod who'd been tormenting an entire kingdom adjacent to Chalmys's own. No big deal, right? *Klerifeg defeated, stronghold destroyed, site cleared for the former village to be rebuilt.*

When would he get to the curse? There was only one page left, so unless he'd said little about his life after... Then she spotted the note scrawled halfway down the last page, and with each word she read, a smile spread ever-wider across her face. He'd stopped before he finished so he could send it to her before she left. Really, if his handwriting was anything to go by, he'd been rushing long before that.

Come to think of it, he'd been visibly disheveled when he sent the scroll through, but she'd been too distracted to ask about it. Had he spent most of the last two days on the task? The mental image of the powerful mage bent studiously over some fancy desk was both endearing and...hot, honestly. Dammit, what was wrong with her?

Holly grabbed an empty folder from her desk drawer and resolutely tucked the papers inside. The parchment hung over the edges of the folder a little, but it would still work better than trying to roll it all back up. For one thing, it would be far easier to pack in her carry-on. A scroll would only get smushed.

When she got to Max's place, she could write down her thoughts on how Chalmys's story should be arranged. It would be a good idea to make note of any holes—such as his childhood—and write out her questions for him. She would just have to keep her sad, neglected libido in check in the process.

Just as she finished tucking the folder into her carry-on, Violet ran back in waving a piece of paper. "I got a few done! I did my best to spell everything right, but you might have to help me fix some."

Holly smiled. Considering her daughter was asking about stuff a little beyond the average Kindergarten curriculum, probably most of it would need correcting if Chalmys hoped to make sense of it. "Let's take a look."

At her desk, Violet crawled up into her lap, and together, they bent over the paper. Half an hour and approximately a million eraser smudges later, the ragged row of questions was finally intelligible. Had her daughter ever worked this hard correcting her school assignments? Maybe she should suggest adding dragons to the first-grade curriculum.

"Alright, love," Holly said. "While you take your bath, I'll finish packing and get all of our luggage in here for the morning."

Violet gave her a quick hug and then jumped down. "I can start the water myself."

Generally true, but Holly trailed behind her daughter to make sure everything was in order just in case. And once Violet was happily sloshing her bath toys around the tub and singing to herself, Holly left the bathroom door cracked open before setting to work. Only a few more clothes for Violet, along with a back-pack of toys and books for the plane trip. The tablet loaded with (mostly) educational games went into the padded bag with Holly's work laptop. Four pieces of luggage to navigate, but doable.

She'd just set the last piece on the couch when an uneasy feeling tickled up her spine. Was something wrong? She headed toward the bathroom, even though she could hear her daughter's humming over the sound of the draining tub. Then the humming ended sharply with a yelp, and Violet hurried out the door with her hair still dripping onto her nightgown.

"Mama, I heard something hit the window." Wrapping her arms around Holly's waist, Violet stared up at her with wide eyes. "Like when I was playing goff and the ball hit the back door."

Normally, she would have laughed at the memory of three-year-old Violet's face when she'd hit the plastic golf ball hard enough to crack against the storm door, but not now. Not when that tingle was now a tap-dancing squad doing a recital on her spine. Was someone trying to break in?

Or had Dylan finally decided to cause trouble?

CHAPTER 14

The alarm jerked Chalmys from sleep so abruptly that he'd gathered a defense spell into his palm before he registered the cause. *Holly?* Though he couldn't fully scry here, he did a quick mental probe for confirmation. Yes—someone had breached the shields around Holly's house.

He shoved his hair out of his face and swung his legs over the side of the bed. Cool stone chilled his feet as he grabbed his discarded robe from where he'd draped it and tugged it on. Then he slipped into his low boots and strode from his bedroom. Although his workroom would be quicker for scrying, he found himself half-running through the back corridors leading to the gardens.

He'd designed the portal stones to create a link between the two worlds no matter where he happened to be, but that was mostly to save energy. If this confrontation turned out to match Holly's brother's dream, then the circle would be best. He would be able to keep the portal spell more stable, and he could channel extra energy to a counterattack.

After activating the lanterns ringing the stone circle, Chalmys flicked two crystals toward the center of the circle, catching them in their proper place with his magic. He activated the octahedron first, and while the scrying link locked into place, he gathered energy around the second stone—the one that held the portal. Only a press of that energy, and the gate would spring to life.

After a deep breath, Chalmys slipped into the ley line. Like earlier, it didn't take him long to find the path to Holly's home. A deeper darkness covered the area, the night more progressed than before. But unlike then, a man holding a rock stood in the yard beside Holly's house. Now that Chalmys had seen Dylan, it was obvious even in the dark that this was him—and his energy matched that of the stranger who'd once wandered by the house.

With a sudden, jerky movement, the scoundrel tossed the rock at one of the windows. It missed, but the thud against the side of the house couldn't possibly have gone unnoticed. Chalmys hissed in a breath. How should he handle the intruder? Nothing that would cause visible harm, since that could create trouble for Holly. A fear spell, perhaps? Though even in that, he would have to be careful, for too much fear could prompt the man into dangerous actions.

The simplest thing might be a wall. Something invisible but difficult to penetrate. When confronted by such an improbable, visually imperceptible obstacle, humans tended to run the other direction until their minds could come up with a reasonable excuse. Yet there was an odd look in Dylan's eyes—disoriented but energetic. Aware but dazed. Could another mage be controlling him? Was he intoxicated? Both would alter his reaction to any spells.

Experience demanded Chalmys show care in a situation like this.

"I know you're in there, bitch," Dylan shouted.

At one of the windows, a curtain twitched. Then Holly appeared, a long, wooden stick in one hand. She lifted the window the barest amount with the other. "What are you doing? Get out of here," she demanded, her anger clear despite her voice being muffled.

"Phone's busted." Dylan's words slurred in an unusual

manner. Intoxication was more likely, then. "I need the money now."

Holly's eyes narrowed. "Are you drunk? Or is it drugs? I bet it's drugs, or you wouldn't be so desperate for money."

"What's it matter to you?" The cur took a stumbling step forward. "Give me the cash, and I'll be gone. Scarlett can have a nice last day of school tomorrow."

"Violet," Holly said through clenched teeth.

"Oh, yeah, whatever." Dylan shrugged. "How about you give me a thousand now and the rest at the first of the month. Gotta replace my phone."

Holly said something about contacting police, but Chalmys stopped paying attention, his focus locked on the intruder. There was something about the way the man stood, his hand tucked in the jacket he wore. Chalmys frowned. A jacket? That didn't match the seasonal clothing he'd observed when searching for additions to the guest room. Besides, he might not be able to feel temperature while scrying, but it was obvious that such thick apparel was out of place. None of the people walking along the streets had worn them.

The man shifted at something Holly said, and Chalmys tuned back into her voice. "Last chance. I have 9-1-1 ready to go."

Her phone was in her free hand now, her finger hovering over the front of it. And in that moment, time seemed to slow. Swaying on his feet, Dylan stumbled a few halting steps forward, pulling something from his jacket in the process. Small. Glinting dully beneath the streetlights. Chalmys might not scry Earth often of late, but even he recognized a gun.

In the window, Holly froze. "Dylan..."

No more delaying. Before the man could raise the gun, Chalmys locked a holding spell around him, freezing the villain's muscles in place. With every speck of his being, Chalmys longed to lance a bolt of lightning directly into the bastard's skull, but a dead body on Holly's lawn would do her no good. If he could ease the situation otherwise, then he would.

He would have to save true punishment for another time.

❧

HOLLY'S HEART pounded a frantic beat even as her focus sharpened on a single point.

He'd brought a gun. An actual gun. Not a knife, like in Gavin's dream. Dylan had somehow bought or stolen a gun, and he'd brought it here to threaten her. Or kill her. She never would have expected... *A gun.* The word repeated in her head to the beat of her pulse. Dammit, she needed to think.

Dylan wasn't moving. He didn't lift the weapon or make more demands. He simply remained in place, his body tilted slightly as though he'd frozen mid-sway. What kind of drug was he on? She searched her memory for any mention of such strange side effects, but her knowledge of illegal substances seemed a bit too limited.

What should she do? If she pressed the call button, Dylan would shoot her before the police could arrive. And Violet...she was hiding in the hallway, out of sight of the living room window where Holly stood but far too close for safety. He wouldn't hesitate to kill their daughter, or... She shuddered at the thought of the horrors a desperate addict could inflict upon a helpless child. *Not going there.*

"Fine, I'll give you the money," Holly forced through numb lips. "Every month. No need for violence."

She could get the police involved once the danger was past, right? Maybe. Possibly. Except...there were too many stories about women shot by exes despite restraining orders and arrest warrants. And the local police force was already overextended, so it wasn't like they had time to give her additional protection. A security system might help. But one slip in vigilance, and boom. Dead.

Oh God, Oh God. She couldn't go up to Max's house, not now. Dylan might not be able to afford a flight, but if he was desperate enough to pull a gun on her, who knew what he might do? A wild road trip wasn't out of the question. He probably didn't know where her brother lived, but how could she be sure? He shouldn't have known about Violet's school schedule, either.

And why wasn't he answering her?

"Dylan, I'm not lying," she said. "Put the gun away, okay? I can't give you money every month if I'm dead."

Holly shivered at the word "dead," and the baseball bat wobbled in her hand. Not that it would do much. Bringing a bat to a gun fight was even worse than bringing a knife. Well, probably. Neither one was going to stop a bullet, was it?

Ping, ping, ping.

She jumped at the little tinkle of sound, fear spinning through her head in a dizzying spiral. Until she processed the source. Chalmys. He was near. Had the protections he'd mentioned been activated?

At the now-familiar nudge against her mind, Holly opened her thoughts to the mage at once. *"Oh thank god Chalmys,"* she sent his way in a rush.

"I have him paralyzed with my magic," the mage whispered into her head, his voice soothing like a balm. *"Aside from bodily functions, he will be unable to move until I release him. Would you like me to kill or otherwise disable him? I suspect not, but the choice is yours."*

Holly shivered. *"I'm not sure I like how easily you mention killing."*

"I am of a different culture with different laws and social conventions," he answered calmly. *"Here, death is an acceptable punishment for one who threatens the innocent, though it is not one I generally prefer. Since we are in your land, however, the choice is yours."*

For one breathless moment, temptation nearly overcame her as her gaze locked on the gun dangling from Dylan's frozen hand. He was such an asshole—and apparently violent, besides. Done carefully, he could be gone from her life forever without any repercussions. But...was that the kind of person she really wanted to be? His choices would be stripped from him, including the ability to choose something better.

If he would. Not even prison or rehab might straighten him up. But there wasn't a way for her to know that for sure, was there? Life or death—she couldn't decide such a thing so casually. *"Don't kill him,"* she replied. *"Just make sure he doesn't hurt us."*

She sensed the mage's assent before his mind withdrew from hers. But at least now, she didn't feel alone. He wouldn't let Dylan hurt them while she figured out what she wanted to do. Not that it was easy. Each time she thought of it, her mind replayed the moment when he'd pulled that gun from his jacket.

Maybe what she needed was to escape, if only temporarily. To take herself and Violet to safety. When her mental image—Dylan overcoming the spell quickly enough to shoot her—couldn't possibly come true, the decision would surely become clearer. And she could discuss other possible solutions with Chalmys.

With Chalmys.

Of course. There was his offer of shelter, wasn't there? Dylan might know where her family lived, but he would never be able to track her to another world. She could send a warning text to her brother, then take Violet somewhere Dylan would truly never find them. A risk? Absolutely. But the possibility of ending up on the news because her asshole ex murdered her and her family seemed alarmingly greater. That shit happened all the time.

A little diversion for good measure wouldn't hurt.

"I guess you're just going to stand there, huh?" She cleared the emergency number from the keypad on her phone. "I don't know what drugs you're on, but get off them."

Holly jerked the curtain closed. Her heartbeat drummed in her ears as she forced herself to walk to the center of the room, her back to the window. *Chalmys better not be lying about Dylan being frozen.* But then, she could only hope he wasn't lying about a lot of things.

Her fingers trembled as she typed out a message to Max and hit send. "Come on, Violet," Holly called out, returning the phone to her pocket. "I texted my friend Amy to come pick us up for the night."

Her daughter poked her head around the edge of the door-frame. "But you don't—"

Holly shook her head frantically, then put her finger to her lips. "I know we were supposed to go to Uncle Max's house tomorrow, but something came up. Amy will probably let us stay with her until we can figure out a new vacation spot. Maybe we'll fly down to the beach."

Violet's expression crumpled into a mishmash of sadness and confusion—naturally, since Holly didn't have a friend named Amy. She pointed her thumb back toward the window, still covered by the curtain. She'd left the window cracked so that Dylan could hear, but hopefully, he wouldn't realize she'd done it on purpose.

"Let's go wait in the kitchen, sweetie," Holly said, tiptoeing to the couch. As quietly as she could, she slipped her backpack onto her shoulders. Then she slung Violet's backpack over her arm and lifted their suitcases, one in each hand. "I'll make you some hot chocolate while we wait for Amy."

Poor Violet trudged into the kitchen, her bare feet slapping angrily on the linoleum. "Mama, I don't like this."

Slumping beneath the weight of all she carried, Holly released a long, tired sigh. "Just bear with me, baby. I think you'll be happy with how things turn out."

Or so she hoped.

Holly sat one of the suitcases down so she could pull the little crystal pendant from beneath her shirt. It was such a clear-but-lovely thing. So delicate to hold so much supposed power. Would it work, or was she a gullible fool?

She took a deep breath and then lifted the stone to her lips.

This was it. No taking it back.

"Chalmys," she whispered, her lips brushing against the smooth, warm crystal.

And the world flashed white.

SHE DID IT. She used the portal stone.

With his awareness mostly centered through the scrying spell, Chalmys scrambled to re-shift his attention, all while the portal flickered and flared. But within the span of several sharp, frenetic breaths, his focus was more properly split. He tightened the energy he'd placed around the second crystal, strengthening the link. Then flexing his magic, he widened and steadied the portal until it was as solid as the archway linking the sections of his gardens.

Wide-eyed, Holly and Violet stared at him from the other side. Had Holly activated the spell by accident? If she'd spoken his name near the necklace in just the wrong way, it was certainly possible, though he'd done his best to safeguard against it. With her expression blank, he couldn't tell what she thought about the open portal, either—but it didn't appear that she was eager to cross to his realm.

Disappointment pinched at his insides, yet he didn't call across for her to join him. Though his laws decreed that it had to be her choice, that wasn't what froze the words in his throat. No, it was fear and honor and pride, for himself and for her. No matter how things proceeded between them, he would never have her feel that he'd coerced her.

What am I thinking? There's only one way for things to proceed, and that's with her acting as my bard, he reminded himself, fighting down the bitterness.

Chalmys nearly asked if she'd opened the portal by mistake. But before the words broke free, Holly gave her daughter the handle of a bright, pink-and-purple-striped trunk, took the child's other hand in hers, and walked them both through. His heart jerked so hard that he nearly lost control of the scrying spell, though thankfully, the portal remained secure.

He never would have forgiven himself if something had gone wrong with that.

Once both ladies were well and truly through, Chalmys met Holly's gaze. "May I close it?"

She licked her lips—an eternal motion to his heart—before finally answering. "Yes. Please close it behind us."

Nodding, Chalmys caught the threads of the spell in his fingers, twisting and unwinding with practiced ease. The spell collapsed back into the two stones where he'd embedded it, one around Holly's neck and the other spinning above the octahedron. He plucked his crystal from the stream and tucked it back into the proper pouch. Now, he need only finish with Dylan.

"One more moment," he murmured.

If either of his guests answered, he didn't know it. His full focus returned to Holly's house where he held her ex-lover bound. Since she didn't want the man injured, Chalmys had to satisfy his ire by toppling the frozen man over with a nudge of magic. Not that the action was merely for retribution. An apparent human statue in Holly's side yard would have drawn the notice of any passers-by. The pest would be more difficult to discern now.

Before withdrawing, Chalmys set the parameters of the spell. It would fade naturally by dawn, yet if anyone touched the man, the magic would disperse at once. Otherwise, if a human happened to see him and attempt to help, there would have been a stir over his locked muscles and inability to move. No need to create a mystery for Earth's healers.

He studied Dylan again, searching for anything he might have missed. Hmm. Should he nudge the villain into unconsciousness? It would be a kindness, but he retreated without doing so.

Such scum didn't deserve relief.

CHAPTER 15

Dream encounters. Glimpses through the mini-portal. Neither had prepared Holly for the reality of him. Nothing could have, honestly. For an embarrassingly long time, she hadn't been able to do anything except stare at him through the gate her necklace had opened. She hadn't even had the presence of mind to snap a picture of him, standing like a movie character in a lantern-lit circle with magic flowing around him in a sunburst of colors. Only a poke from Violet had returned her to her senses.

How could she ever describe the very *presence* of him, though? The power and grace in his motions as he lifted a hand toward the portal at her back? Ah, the way his dark hair slid lovingly around his shoulders and his robe swayed around his legs. A robe that he'd neglected to tie, leaving it to gape open at his neck. To touch that delectable vee of chest...

Good grief. She couldn't even think in complete sentences. He'd asked for a moment, but in truth, she was the one who'd needed it.

"What's going on, Mama?" Violet whispered.

Holly's cheeks heated. She should have been comforting her daughter, not ogling Chalmys while he worked. Even if he *was* ridiculously hot. Hoping he hadn't noticed, she set down her suitcase and knelt at her daughter's side.

"Remember the mage who sent me that scroll?" Holly asked, trying for a reassuring smile. "Do you recognize him?"

Violet rolled her eyes. "Yes, I know Mr. Chamiss. But why are we *here?*"

"*Chal*mys," Holly pronounced carefully. "Mr. Chalmys invited us to stay at his home while I complete the assignment."

"What about Uncle Max, though?" her daughter asked, a frown creasing her brow.

"There was a bad guy outside our house." God, she hoped Violet didn't ask if it was her father. "So Mr. Chalmys let us come here instead. We can still go see your Uncle Max later in the summer, okay?"

Holly held her breath as her daughter processed those words. Would she be too afraid? But resilient Violet merely glanced around the strange stone clearing where they stood, and in a heartbeat, curiosity replaced the last hint of fear in her eyes. Holly could understand why once she took a closer look herself, because...yeah, this was no normal clearing. It was more like a smooth, circular patio. If one's patio was carved with countless mystical designs, at least.

Tall, lantern-topped columns of stone rose at the four cardinal points, and around the perimeter of the circle, a ring of rune-looking designs glowed, golden lines stretching from some of them back to a central point. And above that center, a crystal spun in mid-air. While she could have tried to tell herself that it was suspended on a string, that seemed sort of pointless. She'd never been one to deny reality, and she had *really* walked through a portal that appeared in her kitchen.

Not much of a stretch to admit that this was true magic.

"If there's not a unicorn here, there isn't one anywhere," Violet whispered in an awe-filled voice.

Her daughter was nothing if not persistent. "Do *not* wander off in search of them," Holly warned. "I don't mean this to sound scary, but this is a different world. We shouldn't go anywhere without checking with Mr. Chalmys. He can tell us what and *where* is safe."

Violet's hand wrapped around hers. "Okay."

Holly hated the worry that crept back into her daughter's expression because of the warning, but it couldn't be helped. Her poor, sweet baby. Despite her enthusiasm for magic and mystical creatures, she was still just a child. Holly kissed Violet's forehead and then stood, though she didn't let go of her daughter's hand. She would give her child all the support she needed for this adventure.

Suddenly, the light shining from the middle crystal winked out, and its rotation slowed until it hovered unmoving in the air. Chalmys grabbed the stone and shoved it into a pouch at his waist. Then while the glow faded from the runes beneath their feet, he turned the full force of his attention on them. She couldn't even see the mesmerizing color of his unusual eyes, but it didn't matter. She was captured by them anyway.

He approached slowly, but although he smiled at Holly, it was her daughter he knelt beside. "Good evening, young Violet. I hope you're not afraid to be at my home."

"Was that...?" Violet's grip tightened on Holly's hand. "Was that really magic? Like...real magic?"

Chalmys smiled, and something deep inside Holly cracked. If she were foolish, she might worry it was her heart. "It was indeed," he said. "But I assure you that I use my power to protect and not to harm. This is a safe place."

"Mama said it could be dangerous to wander off."

"Yes, it could be," Chalmys replied matter-of-factly. "The forest on the outer bounds in particular. However, I have made sure you cannot reach any location that could cause you harm, and nothing bad can enter here. But to be safe, do not attempt to go beyond the gardens if you leave the house."

Violet perked up enough to grin at him. "We're not in a house."

The mage laughed as he stood. "So we're not. If you'll follow me, I'll show you to the guest rooms. I believe..." He frowned down at Violet's feet. "Hmm. It seems you had to leave without your shoes, but the path is not always smooth enough to go barefoot. Ah, well, I suppose that's solvable."

"I can—" A flash of light interrupted Holly before she could mention the sandals in Violet's suitcase. Which apparently, they didn't currently need. A pair of purple slippers—in the fairy tale sense of the word—now sat on the ground in front of her daughter's feet. "Okay, then. Never mind."

Surprisingly unafraid, Violet stepped into the shoes and then did a little dance. "They're cozy. If they had pink unicorns, they'd be perfect."

"Maybe later," Chalmys said. He waved his hand, and the suitcases rose a foot off the ground. "Shall we go inside? I suspect more than one of us is ready for sleep."

Holly stared at the carry-on floating in front of her. *You accept reality, remember?*

She met Chalmys's eyes. "Maybe I *could* use some sleep."

CHALMYS HADN'T EXPERIENCED this much anxious excitement since his training years. *Anticipation. It's called anticipation.* Yet that felt like too simple a word. How could the shaky sensation of nervousness blend so well with the buoyant feeling of happiness? Yet it did, especially as he turned the doorknob and gestured for the ladies to precede him into the guest room.

Holly and Violet made it a few paces in before coming to an abrupt halt. Once again, Holly's expression was difficult to read, but her daughter's wide-eyed wonder was clear. Would the child like her own room so well? He concentrated on settling their small trunks beside the bed so he didn't reveal himself by asking such questions.

As he turned back to them, Holly spun in a slow circle, her

gaze sweeping around the entire room. A soft glow dawned on her face, the muted form of her daughter's obvious wonder. Did she recognize the room from the half-formed vision he'd created in her dream? Even then, she'd found it acceptable, so perhaps the complete reality would suffice.

Even if he hadn't had time to figure out her laptop plug dilemma.

"This is gorgeous," she said. "If this is where guests stay, I can't imagine what *your* bedroom must be like."

"I'll be happy to show you sometime," he said. Pink flared in her cheeks, and only then did it occur to him what his words might imply. His own cheeks grew suspiciously warm. "During the tour tomorrow, perhaps? I was thinking it might be best to show you and Violet the entire house first thing in the morning so that you'll know which areas are permissible for guests."

Holly gave a shaky nod. "Yes, yes. That sounds great. Really great."

Though he needed to step away, Chalmys couldn't stop staring down at her. She truly was beautiful in person. Not that she hadn't been in dreams, but the image she'd projected had been blurred and muted by her opinions of herself. And while he'd seen her true form when he'd scried her house, there was a haze to what he perceived using that method, too.

Neither of those had accurately captured the true shade of her eyes—the deep, mossy green of bloodstone with lighter peridot striations—or the red-gold undertones in her nut-brown hair. Nor her supple-looking skin, as creamy tan as the sand lining the beaches near the queen's summer palace. And would the full, perfect bow of Holly's lips feel as soft against his as they looked?

"Oh!" Violet called out, returning him to a world beyond Holly's lovely face. "There are doors over here, Mama."

Chalmys forced his gaze away, clearing his throat as he smoothed his hand down his robe to ease the dampness in his palms. Beside the door to the bathing chamber, Violet stared over at them with a curious expression. He stepped back before she could misinterpret the moment. It was merely...different seeing Holly in person. Nothing more than that.

"You'll find a room for bathing through there, young Violet," he said, hoping neither of them noticed the roughness to his voice. "It's shared between this room and your bedchamber, in fact."

The little girl gasped. "There's a room all for me? But Mama's is so big."

He joined Violet beside the door. It was a perfect excuse to avoid meeting Holly's eyes, for the way he'd stared at her had been far too obvious. Did she think poorly of him because of his rudeness? He probably needed to apologize, but he couldn't seem to make his tongue form the words. So cowardly though it might be, he led the way into the bathing chamber and then directed them onward into Violet's room.

Her squeal of delight was sharp enough to cut and facet a gemstone, but the way she bounced excitedly on the bed and tugged the coverlet against her face was worth the twinge of pain. "There are unicorns allllll over it! Ohh, some are the special kind with wings. I've never seen this in a store before. Did you buy it from a fairy?"

"Alas, no," he replied. "I'm afraid I created the design with my own magic."

Violet gasped. "Oh, wow."

As the little girl darted back and forth across the room, exclaiming with excitement over every new detail, Holly eased up beside him. "Thank you. I can't believe you did so much, even thinking we wouldn't come. I feel a little bad about refusing."

Chalmys spun to face her. "Please do not. I didn't mention it on purpose, because I didn't want you to feel obligated. It was a pleasant distraction from the endless days here, not some chore or burden, as was creating the jewelry."

She winced. "I should probably return most of that since you brought us here. I have a feeling you could charge a hefty price for doing that much magic."

"No, there's no need," he said. His feet itched to take a step closer, and his fingers tingled from the urge to touch her—to grip her stubborn chin between his fingers. In consolation? In command? He wasn't sure. "The amount of effort it took to merely *outline* part of my life made it quite clear how unfair I have been concerning payment. I should offer you an entire estate for so much work, not enforced isolation and a handful of jewelry."

Her eyes widened, and her lips parted in surprise. So beautiful. It was madness how much he longed to kiss her. Gripping the sides of his robe so he wouldn't reach for her, he swallowed against the sudden lump in his throat. Why did he get the uncomfortable feeling he would offer her a great deal more than an estate?

Suddenly, Violet danced between them, and a stark white unicorn with a golden horn popped up in front of his face. "Did you make this? There's a whole family of them."

Holly chuckled, though she stifled it quickly beneath a cough. "Personal space, Violet. Mr. Chalmys isn't used to having children around."

Or anyone.

"Sorry," Violet said as she took a step back.

A sigh caught in his throat, but he smiled down at the child despite the melancholy that reminder was settling into his heart. He had to clear his throat before he could speak. "I created the toys with magic, not by hand. I hope they are satisfactory."

"I got an S for satisfactory for talking, so I guess that's good."

He lifted a brow at Holly, who laughed again. "She means the grade on her report card. Schools send those home to show parents how their children are doing."

"I see," he said, though he wasn't entirely clear about the finer points. Like whether an S in that category meant Violet did a good job at talking or at remaining silent. "Well, I hope you enjoy the toys, young one. I'll also be certain to restructure part of the garden for your personal use."

"I didn't know wizards were so much fun," she announced before darting away again.

Holly rubbed at her forehead. "Don't worry. She'll calm down in a little while."

Chalmys studied the little girl currently peeking at the underside of the desk. "I can't decide if her energy is tiring or refreshing."

"Sounds about right," Holly said with a grin. Then her expression sobered once more. "Seriously, though, thank you. I appreciate your kindness."

"It is my pleasure to offer my aid." Chalmys dipped his head in a bow before promptly cursing at himself for the stuffy motion. He didn't wish for her to think of him as aloof. "Do you need anything else before I leave you to rest? Food, perhaps?"

She shook her head. "No, thank you. We had dinner."

"Ah."

They stared at one another until he feared the awkwardness would become a part of him. Blast it. He tore his gaze away so he could think. What else...? Ah, the drinking alcove. He showed her to the hidden panel and pressed a small crystal embedded in the wall. Above a delicate crystal bowl affixed to a narrow counter, a stream of purest water burbled from a spout. Solid, clay cups were lined up to the side.

"You'll not have to venture from the room if you're thirsty," he said.

Holly ran her finger along the counter before turning to study the other walls. "Do I need to worry about other secret compartments?"

"There are a few for storage." Chalmys tapped his finger beside the crystal. "But I have sealed and hidden the activation stones that would open them. If you would like to use any in your room, let me know."

Once again, she politely declined.

He left with a promise to return first thing in the morning, though he would let her sleep if she didn't answer his knock. But just in case the ladies rose early, he cast a small enchantment over the bedroom doors that would notify him if anyone entered or departed. He didn't leave dangerous magic lying about, but the estate was large enough that they could get lost.

Had he ever been so eager to give a tour?

CHAPTER 16

*I*nsistent ringing dragged Holly out of blessed oblivion. Muttering beneath her breath, she slapped her hand toward her bedside table, only to crack her hand against an unfamiliar edge. What...? Then awareness returned. This wasn't her bed, and that wasn't her table. But that sound decidedly came from her phone.

Hadn't she turned it off? Holly sat up, careful not to disturb Violet sleeping beside her. Then she grabbed the phone and swiped to stop the alarm. The illuminated display claimed it was five thirty in the morning, but the window beside the bed showed no sign of morning light. Not that it would be bright by now at home, of course, but it also wouldn't be *this* dark. Either the sun rose later here, or traveling to another world had wrecked her phone's clock.

Out of reflex, she checked for a signal, but there wasn't one. Naturally. If magic could bring her one thing in this moment, she would wish for a way to read Max's answer to her last text. He was surely freaking out, which meant Gavin would also be freaking out. By this point, they'd probably called her parents.

But for some reason, she didn't regret coming here. Not when she'd fallen asleep replaying memories of how sweet Chalmys had been to Violet and how generous he'd been to them both. Sure, he needed her help to escape his curse, but she'd already agreed to do that. He'd had no need to go to such effort. The man had created unicorn toys after a single conversation, for goodness' sake.

Holly turned off her phone—really this time—but she didn't go back to sleep. Instead, she opened her suitcase and quietly unpacked it. After placing the scroll from Chalmys on the desk, she hung her clothes in a fancy wooden wardrobe and grabbed her bag of toiletries. She could see a haze of light beyond the window now, but Violet still slept soundly. If Holly was quick, she could clean up before her daughter woke.

The bathing chamber was a weird mix of different and familiar, but she managed to brush her teeth and start herself a solid shower after tapping for a bit on the crystals embedded beneath the spout. She couldn't really enjoy it, though. Her thoughts kept pinging between Dylan's attempted attack and the strange situation she'd found herself in.

What should she do? She'd been resolved not to risk Violet by traveling to some unknown world, but this place turned out to have been safer than Earth. Could they risk staying here for longer than a few days? She could finish her work with Chalmys much quicker if she did. Goodness knew the man needed it, because this place absolutely echoed with loneliness.

Holly dried off with a long cloth she'd found folded beneath a counter, then wrapped it around herself and tucked it closed. Frowning at her reflection in the mirror, she picked at the tangles in her hair. The fact was, she could be dead now. That gun... She swallowed hard and tried not to think about it.

Yeah, staying here would be safer in that regard. But could she really trust someone as powerful as Chalmys? The man could control forces she couldn't fathom. *So, he could have hurt you already if he'd wanted to,* she reminded herself as she braided her damp hair back. Instead, he'd saved her and Violet from God-knew-what.

If she could just get a message to her family, the decision

would be much easier. She didn't know what she would tell them, but she could think of something. Probably. If all else failed, there was always the truth. Gavin might believe, since he was apparently psychic. His warning about Dylan had been accurate, even if the events had shifted slightly.

She'd just slipped into a gauzy blue sundress when a knocking sound startled her. Her hand darted to her chest, and she pressed against her breastbone as though it would slow her racing heart. *It's not Dylan,* she chanted to herself a couple of times before she could catch her breath. Chalmys had said he would stop by when it was morning, and clear dawn light now shined cheerfully into the room.

Shaking her head at herself, she padded over to the door and opened it a crack. Chalmys stood politely on the other side, this time in a properly donned tunic and pants. Instantly, the tension eased from her muscles, and her hand dropped from her chest. Why was his aura of power soothing instead of fright-inducing?

A true mystery.

"Good morning," she said, then cleared her throat to combat the scratchiness. "I still need to wake Violet. Could you come back in thirty minutes or so? Maybe an hour? Or...something like that. I don't know how you measure time here. Enough to get Violet ready, I guess."

A slow smile softened his eyes. "Take all the time you need. I'll place a trail for you to follow to the dining room."

"It'll be made out of magic, won't it?" she asked a little wryly.

"Indeed, it will," he replied, chuckling. "I'm afraid I have neither string nor bread crumbs in my pocket."

She suspected he could summon either with a spell, but she also wasn't too tired to recognize a joke. "I look forward to seeing what you create, then."

And she did. All through rousing Violet and finding her clothes, Holly contemplated what form that trail would take. Would he be completely extra and do something with unicorns, or would he choose a simple glowing line? He could go rogue and pick some wild design she'd never seen before. Oh, maybe he'd use tamed creatures. Or a disembodied voice.

Or maybe she'd watched too many children's movies.

"I don't want to eat breakfast," Violet complained as she stepped into her new purple slippers. They didn't match the jeans and bright red T-shirt her daughter had chosen, but whatever. "I want to see the magic house."

Honestly, Holly sort of agreed. They'd barely gotten a glimpse of the fae mage's home last night, but she'd seen enough to suspect that it was both gorgeous and immense. And she was absolutely dying to see the varied ways that he'd incorporated magic. If this ended up being a normal house, she would be painfully disappointed.

She had to be responsible, though.

"After breakfast," Holly insisted, smoothing her hair in the tall, elaborately framed mirror beside the door.

Violet huffed, but she followed Holly into the hallway. Along the beautiful wooden floors, a shining strand of purple-and-pink light twisted and twirled, winding its way to the door on the far end. Little sparkles glimmered within like glitter in the sun, so lovely that Holly almost reached out to touch them. Best not to, though.

"My two favorite colors!" Violet exclaimed, tugging Holly's hand. "Let's see where it goes."

Oh, Chalmys was an observant man indeed, for the two shades were very close to the colors on Violet's suitcase. Though he hadn't gone as overboard as she'd thought he might, it was more elaborate than it needed to be. Clearly, the man had been longing for a chance to show off.

Smiling, she followed the thread.

CHALMYS LEANED his elbow against the table and rested his head against his palm as he tried to remember what had happened between the War of Ivory Fields and the commission to aid Prince Elnen with his border problem. Had that been when he'd spent a couple of years visiting his mother at the temple, or had that happened after completing the commission? Both had been relatively short spans of time. But did it even matter? Such precision might not be essential, not for every single moment.

Vier had decreed that someone must be capable of sharing Chalmys's story, but not even the God of Bards recounted every minute detail of a tale. Not even most of the details, really—that would be boring. An overview of the highlights in an entertaining form would surely impress the god more than a dry history.

Or so Chalmys hoped.

Footsteps sounded in the hall, followed by an excited squeal from Violet. Smiling, Chalmys straightened and set his pen on its stand. He'd decided to work on his outline while he waited, but he was happy to put that task aside for breakfast. Not because he was particularly hungry. No, he found himself eager to see how the newcomers reacted to his home.

"This has to be the last door, Mama," Violet said, her voice carrying through the crack as said door opened. "The line ended in that pretty star."

And in that moment, his loneliness ended.

Both ladies smiled as they approached the two plates he'd set out to his right. He'd moved his own out of the way for papers, but hurriedly, he stacked the sheets together and placed them to the side. He would far rather speak to his guests, and so he made a point of returning their smiles as they sat.

"I hope we didn't keep you waiting too long," Holly said. "But the trail you left was lovely."

He inclined his head as he slid his plate back in front of him. "Thank you. I'm happy to hear that you enjoyed it. As for the other, I had work to keep me occupied. It was no bother."

Violet stared at him, aghast. "Wizards have *jobs?*"

"I prefer the word 'mage,'" he replied, though he chuckled.

"And in this case, my work was an assignment from your mother. I was only able to send half an outline to her before."

"Your life has certainly been eventful," Holly said. "No wonder you haven't been able to accurately deliver it through dreams. It would take forever."

And why hadn't he considered *that* centuries sooner? Truly, it was a wonder that the God of Bards had ever tried to be his friend at all, for Chalmys was more oblivious than he'd ever realized when it came to stories and their delivery.

"I've come to see that you're correct." As he shared a smile with Holly, his heart lightened. Though using the gods-provided platter usually evoked conflicted feelings of anger and resignation, he tapped the elaborate silver plate with its shining silver cover without the usual dread. "Now, food. Meals are a curious affair here, since the Council of Gods agreed to ensure my good health during my punishment. Though I do have some standard supplies delivered, I have this for when I don't wish to cook the more complicated dishes."

One of Holly's eyebrows shot up, and Violet's gaze narrowed on the domed silver lid as though it held all the answers to life. "Let me guess," Holly muttered. "It's enchanted, too."

Chalmys grinned. "Yes, but not by me. Even I am not sure how it works, since I hesitate to tamper with the device that delivers my meals. You need only touch the lid and visualize what you would like to eat."

He placed his hand atop the cool metal and pictured his favorite breakfast: a hearty broth soup, a poached egg, a small loaf of nut bread, and a cup of strong, rich tea. The metal trembled for a second beneath his fingers, and as soon as it stilled, he lifted the cover to reveal exactly what he'd imagined. As both ladies gasped, he calmly removed his food and replaced the lid.

"I'm not sure how well this will interpret Earth food, so this might be something of an experiment," he said, sliding the platter over to Holly. "If necessary, I'll help you find a similar food from my world."

Nodding, Holly stared at the cover with nearly the same concentration as Violet. Their identical expressions made his grin widen until his cheeks ached with it. Though her daughter was more verbal in her wonder, Holly seemed to hold her own quiet fascination for his world. It provided a more pleasant perspective than he'd grown accustomed to.

When she lifted the lid, revealing a pile of fluffy, tan squares coated in brown liquid and a small pile of bark-colored disks, Violet clapped. "Good choice, Mama!"

Apparently, that was how the food was supposed to look.

"I guess your gods recognize waffles with a side of sausage," Holly said, laughing softly. "Here, Violet, hand me your plate. There's enough to share."

They settled into their meal, both ladies digging in with enthusiasm. Though there was much to consider, none of them seemed inclined to speak. But it was just as well. He'd never realized how quickly a little girl could eat. He'd barely finished his soup and started on his egg before Violet declared herself full— and that was without pausing his bites for a discussion.

"I'm ready for the tour," the little girl said. "I want to see *every*thing."

Uneasiness stirred in his gut at the way she stretched out that final word. Would she be disappointed about being barred from his workshop after the tour was over? He had several unfinished devices and countless charged crystals in there, all a certain danger for a six-year-old on her own. Not good if she remained intent on experiencing every last inch of the place.

"But you have to stay out of rooms where you're not allowed," Holly said with a stern look. "We shouldn't disturb Mr. Chalmys's work while we're here."

Speaking of which...

He cleared his throat. "Have you given thought to how long you'd like to stay?"

"Well..." Holly tapped her fork absently against a piece of left-over waffle. "That's a good question. I'm considering working here for a month or two since it's summer break, but there's a lot to think about. I don't know how Violet will do, and I need to settle things with my family. They have to be worried already. If we just disappear, they'll be absolutely frantic."

Ah, he'd almost forgotten that possible complication, but he didn't exactly have a family concerned about *his* absence to remind him of such concern. Aside from his mother, who'd died centuries ago, none of his blood relatives had ever acknowledged his existence—if they'd ever known. But Holly had brothers, at least two that he'd heard of, and possibly living parents. They would not be happy if Holly and Violet disappeared here for the entire summer.

Two months.

His heart pounded. A possible two months with them here, filling his sad home with their life. If there was a way he could help that happen, he would employ his full power to do it.

Chalmys concentrated on cutting a slice of bread, though he snuck quick peeks at Holly as he spoke. "I could open a quick portal if you know of a safe location. That way you could communicate with your family."

A thoughtful look crossed her face. "My parents' house, maybe. Though if Dy—I mean, that man is gone, I suppose you could open a gate into my closet. My phone should have enough charge to call them."

"Are phones not pocket computers?" Chalmys tried to recall what he'd learned of the things. He'd seen written messages. But had he ever observed anyone speaking through one? He couldn't recall. "Do you mean it can also summon others by voice?"

She laughed. "You'd be a natural texter, I guess."

And so he spent the rest of their meal enjoying a discussion on the capabilities of the humans' mobile phone devices.

IT DIDN'T TAKE LONG for Holly to decide that Chalmys's house could more accurately be called a mansion. Or maybe a manor in the old-timey sense. The decorations were different, but overall, the place had a similar vibe to the fancy estates she'd seen on movies and shows set in Regency or Victorian times. High ceilings, sitting rooms galore, the requisite old library, and a ballroom with two gold-and-crystal chandeliers. There were even servants' quarters, though those were unoccupied.

Many of the rooms had elaborate woodwork and painted ceilings, too, but unlike an Earth manor, there were no fireplaces. How was the place heated or cooled? She could see no source of it. Lighting was also different. In most rooms, the light fixture consisted of delicate swirls of gold twining down from the ceiling to cup a massive, glowing crystal, though some areas had crystal-topped sconces along the walls instead.

On the second floor, Chalmys stopped beside a wood panel that might have been a door. Unlike every other room, however, there was no knob to open it. Before she could ask why they were here, he pointed out a large, red gemstone embedded in the wall.

"This gem controls entry to my workshop," he said. "If you're looking for me, tap the stone, and if I'm here, I will come to the door. It will only open for me. This room is forbidden without my presence and permission."

He ran his finger along the stone, and the panel slid open. A mage's workshop. Would it be safe to enter? Violet's hand wrapped around her finger, suggesting her daughter was wondering the same thing. Perhaps they were only supposed to peek in from the entrance?

"I will show you inside if you're interested," Chalmys offered. "If not, we can head to the gardens since the third and fourth floors are currently closed off."

Had he forgotten about his bedroom? Well, Holly wasn't going to remind him about *that* after she'd blundered them both into awkward territory by commenting on it the night before. Seeing some kind of mystical workroom would be enough. Why not? He wouldn't let them get hurt, and it wasn't a chance they were likely to have again.

"I would love to see," she said.

At his gesture, Holly followed Chalmys into the room. Violet stuck close to her side, but a quick glimpse showed more wonder than fear on her little girl's face. Normal nerves, then. Holly stuck her own trembling hand inside her pocket lest she be tempted to touch anything before finally allowing herself to really study her surroundings.

It was...almost boring?

On first glance, at least. The room was massive, easily taking up a quarter of the second floor, but it lacked the ornate decorations they'd seen elsewhere. Instead, the walls were plain gray stone, and the floor was age-worn wood. A few long benches and several tables were situated along the walls, with one stone table the only center point to the room.

Then she noticed the shelves on the far end. Countless objects were stacked there, but she was too far away to discern the details. In fact, many of the tables held tools and items, and one glimmered with gold and jewels. Was that where he'd made her payment, then? She could picture him there, bent over the gold with a look of concentration.

"Do you use magic to make things, or do you make things that use magic?" Holly asked.

"Both," Chalmys replied. "Come."

He led them to the table with the gold and jewels, but he picked up neither. Instead, he took a small, V-shaped device from a tray along the side and placed the object atop her nose. Power tingled over her skin a heartbeat before a pair of lenses simply... appeared. Suddenly, she could see the individual striations of color in his eyes. Every shift in shade, from aquamarine to turquoise to amber, was clear to her now.

"I can increase the magnification," Chalmys said.

He held up a deep green stone and then tapped his finger against the device on her nose. She blinked down at the gem.

Though it had looked perfect on the surface, she could see every little crack and flaw in the shining gem now. "Amazing."

"The magnifying loupe is a device that uses magic to work," he said. "Though I suppose I also used magic to create it."

An artisan mage. Holly gripped the lining of her pocket as a reminder not to touch the objects gathered here, because she had a feeling she could get herself in trouble trying to discover what other things he'd made. And Violet... Well, it was a good thing he kept the room sealed.

"I want to see!" Violet called.

At Holly's nod, he removed the device from her nose and placed it over Violet's. It shouldn't have fit, and yet...however he'd enchanted the item, it remained affixed to her child's nose without effort. "Ohhhh," Violet breathed as she stared down at the gem he'd lowered for her to view.

Holly met his eyes. "Thank you for showing us."

Chalmys smiled. "It is my pleasure. And my vanity, I fear. I have a great many creations now that no one has ever seen. Like my scrying table."

She glanced where he pointed—the central table. They were a little closer here, so she could make out a hint of carving on the smooth surface of the stone. Really, it looked a lot like the circle where she'd arrived through the portal, complete with a crystal spinning lazily above the center.

"Is that where you sat during our dream meetings?" she asked.

"Yes," he answered. "As well as other scrying sessions that didn't involve portals."

"What kind of stone is that? A diamond?" It was clear—that was all she could tell.

Chalmys shook his head. "A flawless quartz octahedron. Few things can match it for channeling and storing power."

Violet piped up. "What about this green one?"

"Emeralds can be used for magic, indeed," Chalmys said, his voice gentling to the patient timbre of a natural teacher. "But not the same kind. Emerald is most useful for healing and protection, but it cannot channel energy in its purest, most neutral state."

Unfortunately, he didn't have the *vocabulary* of a school teacher. Violet frowned up at him. "Huh?"

Instead of taking offense, he smiled. "Magic comes from energy, and energy can take different shapes. The same power that becomes light in a lamp becomes something else in one of your phones."

So it resembled electricity? Her curiosity awakened, Holly could have asked a thousand questions about energy, magic, and gemstones, but her daughter's brow was already furrowed in that look she got when new information was close to being too much. There was no need to add additional details to the confusion. She would have to ask him later—maybe after dinner.

"I need to think about that," Violet finally said.

Chalmys nodded. "I expect so. How about we finish the tour, instead? Then we can see about that portal for your mother."

The portal.

Yeah, she didn't want to think about the conversation she would need to have with Max.

CHAPTER 17

After only half a day in Chalmys's world, it felt strange to step into her house again. The carpet cradled Holly's feet nicely, but the air had a stale scent she'd never noticed before. More than that, though, everything seemed flat, like the atmosphere didn't press against her in quite the same way. Maybe it was the absence of magic? She wasn't sure, but it was something.

"This is weird," Violet said beside her.

Maybe it hadn't been her imagination—but then again, they *had* emerged in the stuffy confines of her modest walk-in closet. "I need to air this room out, huh?"

"I guess," her daughter answered dubiously.

Since Chalmys had scried the area and found it clear, Holly opened the closet door and let the bright light pour in. The air that whooshed in with it was a little less stale, but it was still different. She pondered that oddness all the way to her bed, where she pulled out a spare charger. Best to keep her battery as full as possible.

At least electricity shouldn't be different.

"Remember, you'll need to be patient while I'm on the

phone," Holly said as she tapped Max's name on her phone's favorites list.

Violet bounced up and down on the bed. Already restless, of course. "Can I pick out some clothes for you to take?"

"Sure, but—"

Max answered before Holly could tell her daughter not to go overboard with it. "Where the hell are you? Why haven't you been answering?" he demanded.

"I told you I was fine," Holly hedged, though she'd expected the question. "I'm sorry, Max. Everything happened suddenly."

She could practically see her brother dragging his hand through his hair. "*What* happened? All your text said was that you had to go to a friend's house. I know perfectly well that you were coming here to get away from Dylan, so...what?"

"I haven't said much because I didn't want you to go to jail. And then Mom and Dad—" Holly pinched the bridge of her nose. "You didn't call them, did you?"

"No, only Gavin. But I was about to," Max said. "If you were worried about me and jail, then Dylan must have done something bad this time. So spill it."

"He..." She peeked over at the open closet door where her daughter studied one of Holly's shirts with the focus of a television fashion designer. "Last night, a bad man who has been begging for money came by the house. There have been...threats lately, but this time, he had a weapon."

She was pretty sure the expletives her brother muttered were in Old English, but she wasn't going to interrupt his curse-a-thon to ask. "You didn't think anyone should know that Dylan had escalated to this point?" he finally asked—in modern English. "Dammit, Holly. Why aren't you on a plane?"

"He might know where you live," she pointed out. Then she did her best to gloss over how her ex had ended up immobilized on her lawn. Drugs could be to blame, right? "So I laid a false trail and found a friend he couldn't know about."

"If he's stalking you, then who—"

"You're not going to believe it," Holly interrupted. In this mood, there was only so much bullshit her brother was going to buy. "Even though you've made these kinds of stories your life's work."

His breath hissed across the receiver. "Please tell me you're not going to try to convince me that Gavin's dream was real."

"No." Holly watched Violet pitch a shirt through the open portal and winced. "His dream featured a knife, not a gun, and we didn't disappear in a flash."

"A *gun?* That's it, I'm calling Mom."

"Would you stop?" Holly snapped. How had this gotten so out of control? Honestly, she should be better at explanations than this. Putting things into words was her job. "I'm switching to video. Just look, okay?"

She pulled the phone away from her ear before her brother could protest and then hit a button. His face popped onto the screen, and immediately, regret pinched her heart. Max's short brown hair was a ragged mess, and there were noticeable bags under his eyes. He'd probably stayed up all night worrying about her while she'd been sleeping in an enchanted mansion.

Holly shifted the phone for a better angle—the underside of no one's chin looked good. "See? Perfectly safe and healthy. But I'm not the interesting part."

After removing the charging cable, she hurried over to the closet and swung around until her back was to the door. "Holly, this is a waste of—" His eyes widened, and his mouth dropped open. "What the fuck is that? And Violet's just standing by... whatever it... It's not your closet. That is *not* your closet, Hol."

"Don't you have a doctorate?" she couldn't resist asking. "Didn't they teach you how to use words?"

Ah, well. Guilt only went so far compared to taunting a sibling. In just about any situation, apparently.

"You can't show me something like that and expect coherence," Max grumbled. "Would you just explain already?"

Holly did her best, but in this case, her brother's knowledge wasn't to her benefit. The questions. Oh, great God, the questions. What kind of fae was Chalmys, and how had the deal been struck? Had she given him her true name? Did she know not to eat any of the food? What would she do if—if—if—? Her arm was tired from holding the phone long before he ran out of steam.

"Max. I ate breakfast there just this morning, yet here I am, talking to you in the middle of my bedroom the day after I left," she argued. "Calm down."

In the closet doorway, Violet pointed at her foot. "He made me purple shoes. There aren't any unicorns there so far, but I like it anyway. And Chalmys is nice. There's a magic plate that makes waffles. I wish you could visit, Uncle Max. I know how much you love waffles. Maybe someday. There's a pretty garden, and crystals, and magic glasses. You'd love it."

The conversation took longer than she would have liked, but in the end, it was Violet's enthusiasm that won him over. Not that she needed her brother's permission, of course. But convincing him that she would be okay would help the rest of her family be reassured. Well, Gavin, anyway. Her parents were going to remain blissfully unaware while on their anniversary trip.

"Now that you know, I can try to drop you messages," Holly said. "Check your desk every once in a while for a scroll, okay? Obviously, there's no phone tower or internet where I'll be."

"Fine, but I'm not happy about it," Max groused. "There's no way to help you if something goes wrong."

She smiled at her brother. With his rumpled hair and annoyed scowl, he looked exactly like a cranky professor in a rom-com. "As I saw last night, nowhere is really safe, right? I promise I'll send you notes. Maybe Chalmys will even have some interesting myths I could copy over. How great would that addition to a folklorist's research be?"

The gleam of interest in his eyes showed the deal was sealed.

CHALMYS MIGHT BE A POWERFUL MAGE, but even he had his limits. Holding open a portal to an entirely different world for an indeterminate amount of time was definitely one of them. Already, he was coated in a thin sheen of sweat, and his muscles ached from the strain of maintaining his position in the center.

It wouldn't have been so bad if he'd established the spell while Holly was on Earth, her crystal balancing the other side, but he'd only had one of the pair of stones to work with this time. That meant the lack had to be accounted for with his magic. Also not a problem, except that he had to split his focus in order to scry for Dylan. Even using the most basic of scrying spells added to the burden.

And that was before young Violet started tossing clothes through the portal from Holly's closet. He had to sweep each one up and away with his magic, then settle it safely to the side, for if one of the support gemstones were knocked askew, he would have to hold the *entire* weight of the spell with only his power. He simply hadn't had enough rest for that, not after the major spells he'd recently done.

Not to mention how out of practice he was. Really, he'd survived wars with less drain. Perhaps he should consider enlisting the child's aid for training, for she was quite adept at throwing unexpected burdens his way. At the mental image of little Violet chunking stuff at his head while he worked in his practice circle, he smiled. She would probably love it.

Time stretched long like the line of sweat that rolled slowly down his back, leaving his skin itchy in its wake. He could use magic to erase the sweat, of course, but such a spell required more energy than he was willing to expend. So he did his best to ignore the discomfort, sweeping away flying clothes and holding the portal with his resolve despite the unpleasant sensation.

He sighed with relief when Holly swept into view, but she merely turned her back to the portal and held her phone high in front of her. The conversation was a difficult one, then. He'd given her permission to reveal the portal to her brother if necessary, though the location and appearance of Chalmys's home were secrets he guarded from humans in nearly every circumstance. Even from those with latent fae blood—or maybe especially those.

But considering the situation, sharing such information was reasonable. He would be a cruel man to leave her family ignorant with Dylan such a threat. Now, whether they would believe what they learned... Who knew? Modern humans found the most convoluted ways to deny any information outside of their limited expectations.

By the time Holly and Violet walked back through, Chalmys was ashamed to admit that his muscles trembled from the strain. It had only been, what, an hour? Less than two. He truly was growing soft. Innate energy capacity was one thing, but using that energy was another. Like muscles, it required exercise, and it seemed he hadn't had enough.

Chalmys closed the portal and the scrying link as soon as both ladies had stepped well away. "How did it go?"

Holly's nose wrinkled. "It took a lot of talking, but I finally got Max calmed down. I might have bribed him with some unique legends from your library, though. I hope you really have some of those."

"I do," Chalmys said as he reclaimed the crystals he'd used for the spell. "If he's interested, I can also list the tales that were supposed to be based on my life. I suppose a scholar could make something interesting out of those centuries of failure. I assume you've agreed on a place to send him messages?"

"Yeah, I—" Holly groaned. "Violet! How many of my clothes did you throw through the portal? I thought it was only one or two."

As Holly frowned at the uneven heap of clothing, the faux-innocent look on the little girl's face made Chalmys feel unaccountably like a co-conspirator. "Mr. Chalmys made a pile for me. Wasn't that nice?"

And that sealed the feeling.

"Except for the part where you just tossed them in. What if that had messed up the portal?"

"I'm sorry, Mama." Violet's expression was as sweet as her morning waffles. "I know you didn't pack much, and I wanted you to look pretty. And anyway, I didn't want to wander off in case the bad man came back. It got boring in there."

Holly closed her eyes and took a deep, audible breath. Then she smiled down at her daughter. "I guess it doesn't matter, since Mr. Chalmys doesn't seem mad."

With a shaky hand, he swept a few strands of hair off his damp forehead before offering a tired smile of his own. "It made for good exercise. Violet would be an excellent assistant for a combat mage in that regard."

Holly winced, but the little girl's eyes lit with joy. "Thanks, Mr. Chalmys!"

Chuckling, he used his magic to lift the pile of clothes. "How about we get these to your room?"

It was perhaps an unnecessary strain to use his power for the task when they could carry the clothes between them, but it would ease their walk. He would do a million times more work to keep them happy here, energy depletion or no.

Which was why he returned to his workroom as soon as he left Holly and Violet sorting clothes in Holly's room. He might need rest, but there was one dilemma he still needed to solve—the computer charger. He'd made note of how she'd renewed the battery on her phone, and he suspected he could replicate the effect with properly channeled magic. However, research was paramount, especially with the memory of Dylan's burning phone fresh in his mind. Holly would not be pleased if he set her working device aflame.

With that reminder, he merged into the ley line and prepared for a long research session.

UNFORTUNATELY, Chalmys didn't have as long as he would have liked. He was deep in a scan of various Earth batteries when the summoning bell resonated in his gut, pulsing with the unpleasantness of a poorly cooked meal. Hissing out a curse, he returned his awareness to his workshop and shoved away from the scrying table. He hadn't shown Holly and Violet the communication room, but Vier would make *sure* he didn't forget about it.

Chalmys hadn't thought it possible, but he activated the link with even less patience than the last time. "I told you they might be coming."

"Hello to you, too, old friend," Vier drawled. "I believe I told *you* I would be watching your little realm, and I'm concerned by the number of portals being opened. As well as the presence of a child, of course, but you made your point clear about that."

Chalmys's lips thinned. "I have obeyed every stipulation of my confinement. What is this really about?"

"This is taking too long," Vier replied, an odd note to his voice. "You've been confined for so many centuries that Prince Kleress is nearing his accession. He'll be formally named Crown Prince next month. Could you *please* entrust *this* bard with your story so that you can be freed?"

Had the god really just...? Fingernails biting into his palms, Chalmys glared at the communication stone. Yes, centuries had passed, certainly enough that his grandmother was preparing to transfer power to his father. An entire dynasty of years gone. And who was responsible for that?

"You're the one keeping me here," he protested.

"Not at this point. Once set, a god's curse can't be easily removed, even by the one who placed it. I *never* imagined you would be so dense." Vier hesitated, the silence growing more charged between them. "Chalmys, your true story must be known. By you. By everyone. This latest bard might not be fully fae, and she certainly isn't one of my disciples. But she's good enough to do this. If you let her. So *let her.*"

The link cut off, and for a moment, Chalmys had to bury the

urge to smash the communication stone against the wall. That absolute bastard had the nerve to sound regretful. And chiding. As though Chalmys wanted to be stuck here. As though he was simply inept. But he couldn't tell the god the true problem without betraying his mother.

She might be dead, but her soul resided with the goddess she'd served. That peace was her reward as a priestess. But the gods of his realm weren't omniscient, not as they often were in human legends. Since his mother hadn't been caught breaking her vows, she'd received no punishment.

A wrong word from Chalmys would irrevocably change that.

He pressed his palms against his eyebrows and breathed through his nose. There had to be a reason Vier was pressuring him now when decades could usually pass between them speaking. Why would the god be so anxious to have him free? Was there trouble brewing?

Well, whatever it was, Chalmys wanted no part of it.

CHAPTER 18

After a couple of days of floundering, Holly and Violet settled into a routine. They had breakfast and dinner with Chalmys, but lunch depended entirely on whether he was holed up in his workshop. In fact, she'd had to tap on the crystal outside his workroom on the first day to ask if she could use the platter for Violet's lunch. He'd looked more tired and annoyed than she'd seen him before, but he'd helped her figure out the meal without complaint.

The day after that, Chalmys had rearranged a surprisingly large portion of his garden to create a place for Violet. It was an outdoor wonderland, with a series of fun-but-simple hedge mazes, a sand box, and even a little play cottage, complete with furnishings. Holly had spent the rest of the afternoon enjoying the sight of her daughter exploring every inch of the place.

But after that, she forced herself to focus on her work. Chalmys had given her permission to spread out her research on one of the tables in his library, a glorious room full of ancient-looking books. She'd had to warn Violet to ask permission before grabbing any of those, though—some of them were probably older than human civilization. Instead, her daughter set up elaborate stories with her unicorns along the empty tables. Today, there was a battle to see which unicorn got to be the Queen of Ice Cream.

But even though things were going well on the surface, Holly couldn't shake the feeling that something was up with Chalmys. He was as friendly and kind as always, but there was an edginess to him that bothered her. She'd even asked if he was upset by the disruption to his schedule, but he'd adamantly denied that. Maybe he was simply worried about breaking his curse?

Although if that were the case, repeatedly evading her questions about his birth and early years was an odd choice. A suspicious choice, actually. She tapped the end of her pen—an *enchanted* pen with magically renewing ink—against her paper. Could he be hiding something? She'd thought it was the scope of his life or the methods he'd used with others that had caused earlier attempts to fail, but maybe it wasn't that. If he wouldn't share the details, she couldn't tell his story.

Suddenly, Violet flopped across the empty side of the table and let out a dramatic sigh. "I'm bored."

"What about the Queen of Ice Cream?" Holly asked.

"She was crowned. She promised there'd be ice cream for everyone." Her daughter's second sigh ruffled the edges of Holly's notes. "Now what?"

"New trouble in Unicorn Land?"

Violet frowned. "That is not what it's called, Mama. Anyway, I'm tired of being stuck in here. I want to go play in the garden."

Holly hesitated. Her fear didn't make sense on the surface—there was no chance of a stranger bothering Violet, and the area was apparently enchanted against any possible danger, including bugs, plants, and animals. Chalmys had even given her daughter a crystal pendant she could squeeze if she needed help. But despite all that, letting her baby run free on another world made Holly's stomach clench with dread.

Sometimes, parenting sucked—because this discomfort was one she would have to learn to accept.

"Please," Violet begged. "I promise I'll stay in the play area Mr. Chalmys made for me."

Holly couldn't think of a single reason not to let her. "Fine, but remember to stay away from the places you're not allowed to go. And you have the necklace if you're hurt or scared."

Violet sprang up and did a little dance of glee. "I know, I know. I just want to run through the maze."

With a nervous smile, Holly watched her daughter skip out of the room. *I can do this. I can do my work. I won't turn into a helicopter parent in the safest place we'll probably ever be.*

But she'd barely made a handful of notes when Chalmys walked in. "Is something wrong?" he asked.

"Not really." She leaned back against her seat. "Okay, maybe. I'm still adjusting to letting Violet roam free, and I'm worried I won't be able to tell your story properly, too. I have so many notes about information I need to fill in."

He pulled out the chair beside hers and sat, his gaze skimming over her papers. His hair was tied back at the nape today, highlighting the point of his ears and the strong line of his jaw, and it was nearly impossible not to stare. She squirmed a little at the unwelcome heat that flushed through her.

"Hmm...you're summarizing well," he said, his low, melodious voice nearly making her shiver. "But I can help, of course. With both problems."

What problems, again? Surely, he hadn't meant he would help with her wayward libido. She couldn't stop herself from glancing at his lips. What would she do if he wanted to kiss her? *No contest. I would totally let him.*

But when Chalmys turned in his seat, it wasn't for an embrace. Instead, he reached into one of the pouches on his belt and pulled out a crystal sphere the size of a golf ball. Gently, he lifted her hand, turning it over until it rested atop his. The feel of her hand cradled in his, warm and steady and comforting, distracted her so much that she barely noticed when he dropped the stone into her palm. God, she really wanted to kiss him.

"Tap it three times quickly, and you'll see Violet," he said.

It took Holly's lust-muddled brain a moment to process his words, but at least some of that heat shifted to an embarrassed blush. Hoping he didn't notice her awkwardness, she tapped against the crystal. Sure enough, a tiny image of Violet walking between the hedges filled the crystal for several moments.

But it winked out quickly. "Is it supposed to do that?"

He nodded. "It would have taken a much greater working to create something longer-lasting, but I thought this would suffice for now."

"It's great." And it really was—this way, she could check on her daughter without becoming obsessive about it. "Thank you."

Though a smile crossed his lips, it lasted about as long as the spell image. "If only the second part of your dilemma was so easy to solve," he murmured. "I've nearly completed the rest of the outline, but the beginning... I fear we'll have trouble with all the holes."

So he *had* been intentionally skimpy on the early details of his life. But why? She studied him for signs of deceit, but there was only pain and grief etched on his face. And with his hand still cupping hers beneath the smooth crystal, she felt more connection than distance. More kinship than suspicion. He simply wasn't the kind of man to hide important information for his own shallow gain.

"Are you going to tell me the problem, or are you going to pretend I'll get by without learning the full truth?" she asked softly.

"It's only..." His hand twitched beneath hers. Then almost reluctantly, he released her, and she cradled her now-cold hand against her chest. "There are details of my birth that should not be known. Revealing those secrets would endanger others, so I'm hoping they can be glossed over."

What did he mean, endanger others? His parents, maybe? It must be, for there was so much pain in his eyes. At the fathomless depths of it, her heart melted—and yet it ached. Yeah, he was *exactly* the kind of man who would spend centuries in captivity for the sake of someone he loved.

"I guess that's what's been bothering you," she said, sighing. "I thought you'd been acting strange for the last couple of days."

"Ah. That." He rubbed the back of his neck. "Vier, God of Bardcraft and my wretched captor, called me through the communication crystal just before your first dinner here. Speaking to him has put my mood askew for days."

The god who'd trapped him could speak to him at will? It made sense, but Holly hadn't expected it. No wonder Chalmys had been upset. "Was it bad news?"

"I...don't know." His brows drew together. "He sounded different. Almost friendly, even as he chided me for not gaining my freedom sooner. He seemed upset that I've been here long enough for the queen to formally crown her heir, and I cannot fathom why. Unless, of course, Kleress wants me at his coronation. It's the only reason I can think of to explain why Vier pointedly mentioned the event."

Holly took a moment to puzzle through those words. Vier: God of Bards. Kleress: a prince of...somewhere. A kingdom close to Chalmys's estate, maybe. But she couldn't begin to understand the motivations behind any of it.

"Is there a reason why this prince would want you there?"

The muscle in Chalmys's jaw twitched, and his gaze fixed resolutely on the stack of papers on the table. Definitely a connection, then, but he didn't seem ready to disclose it.

Until he did.

"Kleress is my father."

HIS THROAT CLOSED AS THOUGH TRYING to strangle off any further revelations. He'd never told a soul that truth—no one. Even his mother had only discussed the matter with him once, just before he'd left for his apprenticeship. That had been a caution, in fact. *You mustn't let anyone make the connection. And for the sake of all, avoid the royal family as much as possible.*

"I'm guessing there's a reason that isn't on this paper," Holly said, poking her finger on the first sheet of his outline.

Chalmys nodded. "A vital one. The secret is so well-guarded that I believe only Prince Kleress himself knows. My mother is no longer alive to speak of it."

"Okay, so…" A hesitant expression crossed Holly's face. "You have a major family secret and a god eager enough to hear your life story that he cursed you over it. Are you sure this god doesn't suspect something?"

Not being a fool, Chalmys had considered that before, but he'd ultimately decided against it. "We were friends at the time. If he'd heard rumors like that, he would have asked me directly to confirm the truth. I'm not certain what I would have *done* in that case, but it never happened. No, the curse was a matter of protocol. As host, I should be willing to offer the same a guest might give. He told me his tale, so I was obligated to recount mine. He thought I was insulting him when I refused."

The corners of her lips turned down, and he had to resist the urge to run his finger across the soft flesh until her usual smile returned. "I don't know your rules of etiquette, but that seems… off," she said. "If you were close enough that he would have asked you about any rumors, then why would he have turned petty over a story? I really think you should consider this carefully, Chalmys. Maybe there's something about this that *you* don't know."

Chalmys, your true story must be known. By you. By everyone. By. You.

He froze, sick dread pinning him to his seat like a holding spell. Could Vier have set him about this task for a different purpose than the one he'd always assumed? But what could there be about his own birth that he didn't know? His features were a solid blend of both his parents, enough that his origins weren't necessarily obvious, yet he could identify characteristics from both. His father's jawline. His mother's sharp cheekbones. The aquamarine of his mother's eyes blended with the amber of his father's. He simply had no doubts about his parentage.

Enough that it was a surprise none of the priestesses had ever called his mother on it.

Swallowing hard, Chalmys cast the tightest shield he could around his estate, ensuring that only he, Holly, and Violet would hear anything within. "My mother, Larah. She was a priestess dedicated to the Goddess of Temperance, and that required a vow of chastity. She lied to bring me back to the temple with her, claiming I was an orphan. If her deception is discovered, her soul could be forfeit."

"Oh." Holly's eyes widened. "Ohhhh."

"Indeed." He smoothed his thumb across the wooden table. A sort of grounding while his world tipped and spun. "Vier claimed to be my friend, so it's difficult to imagine anything but spite in forcing me to reveal something like that."

Holly nodded, but he could almost see the way her thoughts had circled on the problem. Had she seen an angle he hadn't? She'd already brought up a couple of points that he'd rather not consider.

Perhaps Vier had told the truth about one thing: *She's good enough to do this, if you let her.*

HOLLY COULDN'T STOP THINKING about Chalmys's revelation—nor the obvious problems it brought. It would require careful wording to even mention where he was from, and the rest of the story had to flow from that. Could she gracefully glide over such a harsh reality? Simply mention that he'd been an orphan at the temple? That might be enough, since an orphan wouldn't know their parents, anyway.

Unless, of course, this god happened to know the truth.

Her footsteps carried her from the clearing where Violet played and along a stone path lined with trellises, all redolent with roses. But she barely admired them. Instead, her mind played through the possibilities of Chalmys's birth like abandoned cuts from a movie. Scenes where his parents had shared a secret love. Scenes where they'd given into a moment's temptation. Or on the darker end...

She came to a halt in the middle of the path. What had his mother told him about her relationship with his father? Was Chalmys certain she'd been willing? Would it matter? Virginity was lost no matter how it was taken, right? If assault wouldn't count against her vows, then his mother surely would have claimed him.

Holly rubbed at her forehead. Maybe she was searching for a way to excuse the god's actions instead of figuring out a way around the problem.

"I didn't mean to trouble you," Chalmys said softly from behind her.

With a yelp, she spun to face him. She had to take a deep breath to calm her racing heart. "But did you mean to startle me?"

One corner of his mouth tipped up. "Of course not."

There was such a light in him that she could barely tolerate the possibility that he'd been created in a moment of darkness. He would be so very hurt by that. She would far rather it be one of those scenes of star-crossed love.

"Chalmys, I hesitate to ask this, but do you know..." She sucked in another breath and plunged in. "Do you know the story of your parents' meeting? If your mother was unwilling..." His expression went closed and hard. "I'm sorry. I don't know why I was even wondering. The result would be the same."

Chalmys's gaze dropped to the stone path. "In truth, I *don't* know. I never learned such things. I wish I had."

The crack in his voice cut through her until her heart felt as raw as the agony in his eyes. Before she could think better of it, Holly bridged the gap between them, her arms slipping around his waist. He flinched, but before she could draw back, he gathered her close.

It was an innocent embrace, firm and full of comfort. But his warmth seeped into her blood like a drug—and an undefinable *something* clicked into place like a part of her soul. Holly rested her head against his chest. His steady heartbeat lulled her, though the weight of his hand low on her waist sparked her desire to life.

"Does this mean Mr. Chalmys gets to be my new dad?"

Holly startled, knocking her head against his jaw, before taking a step back. A very large step. Though Chalmys chuckled, she couldn't bring herself to meet his eyes. "No, Violet. Mr. Chalmys was sad, so I gave him a hug. That's all."

"Oh." Surprisingly, her daughter's lower lip poked out in a pout. "Maybe someday. So can we have dinner? I'm hungry, and I want to think myself some chicken nuggets on the magic plate. And ice cream. The unicorn queen said I could have some."

"Dinner it is, then," Holly managed to force through her lips.

No, she absolutely wasn't going to meet Chalmys's eyes.

Nor would she admit how much she missed his warmth.

CHAPTER 19

Chalmys studied the device taking shape on the workbench, but it was difficult to keep his focus on it when so many thoughts and feelings circled in his mind. Some pleasant, like the perfection of holding Holly in his arms or the heat he'd seen in her eyes in the library. Others...markedly less so. He'd tried for so long not to wonder about the nature of his parents' relationship, but now he couldn't keep worries about it buried.

Work. He needed to work.

After tucking a stray hair behind his ear, Chalmys settled one of his largest octahedrons in its new copper cradle. He'd determined the proper amount of energy to channel through the crystal and into the copper, and he'd even created a switch Holly could use to turn the flow on or off. But the connection point between the device and her plug was...definitely a work in progress. He would be so much closer if he could just concentrate.

If you were close enough that he would have asked you about any rumors, then why would he have turned petty over a story?

With a sharp curse, Chalmys shoved away from the table. He braced his hands on the edge, his head hanging low as he tried to force the swirling questions aside. But it was impossible. Despite all his mother had confessed to him, there was so much he didn't know about his parents. So much he couldn't answer—like whether she'd been mistreated. She had guarded her secrets so carefully that they should have remained undiscovered, even by the Bard of the Gods.

Now, Chalmys wasn't so sure.

How much did Vier know, and how had he learned it? Had Chalmys slipped at some point, revealing enough for the pieces to be put together? Perhaps he'd betrayed his mother during one of his countless conversations with the god. They'd spent many an hour around campfires after various battles, Chalmys there as a fighter-mage and Vier there to chronicle it all. If Chalmys had been tired enough, he might have given just the wrong details about his life.

But what if there were rumors being whispered, instead? Of all the gods, Vier would know. He would hear and collect. Catalog and ponder. If that were the case, then others had somehow learned the truth. The tale need only make its way back to the wrong god, and that would be that. Maybe Vier had thought to trap Chalmys here for safety, in this place where the curious couldn't examine his features for signs of similarity to Kleress.

It *had* been out of character for the god to cast such a curse. What if Chalmys had spent centuries judging Vier wrongly? Chalmys had said terrible things to his former friend, especially early on. In a sense, that would be deserved regardless—the trap was cruel no matter the reasons—but he would regret it all the same if the god hadn't had ill intentions.

Whatever the case, Chalmys needed to find out. He leaped to his feet and strode directly to the communication room. The large crystal sat in its haphazard spot. Silent. Almost waiting. Before he could change his mind, he activated the stone with a flick of his hand.

It connected almost at once. "Chalmys? Has there been some disaster? You haven't reached out since—"

Since the first decade when he'd called incessantly to beg, plead, or cajole.

Not that it had worked.

"Why are you so determined that I speak of my life?" Chalmys demanded without preamble. "Do you know something I don't? *Why?*"

A terrible, eternal silence. Then... "I stumbled upon a half-dead priestess one night, not long before our ill-fated dinner."

"Was it...?" Blast, he'd almost asked if it was his mother, though at that point in time, it couldn't have been her. "Was it too late to save her?"

Vier's chuckle scraped dry across the link. "That's not what you were thinking, hmm? Alas, the delicate priestess died. She made sure of it, for she was too shamed that she'd fallen for Kleress's lure."

Ice pierced Chalmys's blood at that. For the first time in ages, he wished he could see Vier's face so he could determine the truth behind his words. "You're claiming the prince hurt her, then?"

"I hear his gift of compulsion is quite strong. Curious that he's gaining so much power despite the queen's relative youth," Vier said, a bite to his tone. "Listen, Chalmys. I long ago guessed what you hide and what you fear. But after meeting that priestess... If Kleress enjoys harming others with his wretched blasphemies, his crimes must be revealed."

And Vier clearly believed that Chalmys was proof of one of those crimes.

"You think me a wretched blasphemy?" he asked with a little mirthless chuckle.

"Are you confirming my suspicions?" Vier countered.

Chalmys clenched his hands into fists. "No. I was merely *confirming* how you believe this story relates to me. That seemed to be where you were heading."

"That's not what I meant at all. A person who is coerced is hardly at fault, and a child of such a union would be less so," Vier replied, affront ringing in his tone. "As I have often told Peorban, strict vows of chastity are foolish. Temperance is moderation, not abstinence. She's simply jealous for her followers' attention."

"I don't care about your philosophical discussions with the Goddess of Temperance, Vier," Chalmys snapped. "Why is Kleress *my* problem?"

The god sighed loudly enough for the sound to be heard across the connection. "You're the only mage I've met who is capable of easily resisting his compulsion. And if you *are* the living proof of his assaults on the priestesses assigned to his estates, then it's an additional boon that you're one of the few who can share that truth without being forced into silence. Of course, I'd thought you might investigate your origins in greater detail during a brief captivity, but instead, you've made only the feeblest attempts at sharing what you already knew. Across centuries."

"But—"

"Think on it," Vier said. "I vow your mother's soul will be safe if I have to battle Peorban myself."

As was his dramatic habit, Vier severed the connection without a word of warning. Chalmys found himself grateful more than annoyed, for his thoughts spun too chaotically to formulate any reasonable reply. Vier *had* guessed the truth—and connected it to the violation of another priestess, besides. Chalmys's stomach lurched at the terrible implications.

Had he ever really known anything about his parents at all?

Averting his gaze from the stone, he considered what to do next. Right now. He couldn't possibly return to working on the device, but he also wouldn't be able to sleep. Not like this. He strode from his workshop as though on a mission, but his pace was driven more by his emotions than anything else. He had to do something to purge himself of the turmoil that froze and burned his blood in equal measures.

The lights he passed were muted, the house silent. It had to be nearing the moon's zenith, so Holly and Violet would have long ago gone to bed. But he could feel them there, that faint aura that lingered in the presence of so much life. When he slipped out the door to wander the paths, even the gardens still echoed with it.

He had no clue how long he walked, but the moon was still high overhead when he reached the edge of the forest. A section of the woods had been trapped in isolation with him, and if he went far enough, he could find the glimmer of Vier's wretched shield within. The unicorns lived near there, and more than once over the last couple of days, he'd considered trying to tame one for Violet.

With an enchantment, he could at least bring one close enough to observe, and night would be a good time to experiment. A diversion, if nothing else. Chalmys took a step onto the forest path, but his feet refused to move further. What was he thinking? No, he couldn't do it. He couldn't shatter her beautiful dreams with the harsh reality of these beings' true nature. Gods knew life would bring her enough of that.

He spun on his heel and wandered back into the gardens. Too bad he couldn't deny his own reality, no matter how hard he'd tried. He'd avoided Kleress, hadn't he? Kept to his duties as a mage without interacting with the royals. But had that avoidance caused greater harm? He would have noticed compulsion magic if he'd been near it. He might have saved the priestess Vier had found if he'd stopped the prince from using such dark power centuries ago.

No. Not my fault.

He would not claim his father's crimes as his own.

Still, being aware of the possibility meant that Chalmys had a responsibility in the present. While he couldn't ask his mother for details, there was every chance she'd left the information behind. She'd kept countless journals over the centuries, mostly devotional. He'd skimmed through a few after receiving them upon her death, but reading her words when his heart had already been hollow with loneliness had been too much.

Yet he would have to bear it now—it was his only chance to learn the truth. If his father had used coercion, he certainly wouldn't admit to it. At this point, Chalmys had to hope that his mother had dared to leave him *anything* about his birth, no matter how painful it happened to be. She might have raised him —it wasn't uncommon when a priestess brought back an orphan —but she'd held his true origins a tight secret, almost never discussed.

Finally tired, he turned down the path lined with roses where he'd found Holly earlier. It was a good memory, having her in his arms. There was something about her...some essence that called to him deeply, but her warm nature and quick wit had won him over all the more. She, too, had been through much, but she hadn't let it dampen her spirit.

A ghost of a smile crossed his lips at the memory of young Violet's interruption. He'd been touched by her innocent question—and proud of it, too. Not that he deserved the honor of her easy acceptance, of course. What had he done besides make a few toys and alter his garden a little?

But her approval had pleased him all the same.

⁂

HER DAUGHTER HAD FINALLY BEEN comfortable enough to sleep in her own room, but Holly found herself tossing and turning in her bed like an antsy child. She couldn't seem to stop her mind from puzzling over the mysteries of Chalmys's life—or replaying that embarrassing moment in the garden. As soon as she got her thoughts shifted away from one, they slid right over to the other.

With a huff, she sat up, her gaze sliding around the moonlit room. Not much distraction here. She'd already explored every bit of it, including the storage cabinets that opened at a touch. They'd all been empty, not even spare bedding or forgotten dust bunnies filling the space. Well, with one exception—the dressing room had held a few tall closets with a variety of Earth-style clothes inside.

The man had gone shopping for her. With magic, anyway.

Holly padded across the cool wooden floor to the window. Moonlight gilded the gardens that stretched below, and in the distance, she could see the silver-tipped trees of the forest. Near the edge, she spotted the stone circle where she and Violet had emerged. It was quiet now, only the glimmer from above lighting the gray rock with its glow. In her mind's eye, though, she could still see Chalmys directing his magic with ease.

Until her trip back to Earth. He'd actually looked tired after that one.

Movement caught her eye, and she squinted down at the rose-lined path that had featured in her memories tonight. Was someone...? Ah, it was Chalmys. Why was he walking this late? Had he had trouble sleeping, too? But the longer she stared, the more concern picked at her. His shoulders sagged, and he kept tugging his hand through his hair. Maybe she'd really upset him with her questions about his past.

Spinning away, Holly snatched up her robe and tugged it over her thin pajamas. Then she paused to tuck her Violet-observing crystal into her pocket and slip into her sandals before crossing to the door. Maybe it was silly, rushing out to comfort a fae mage who'd survived centuries without her help, but she couldn't stop herself from doing it anyway.

She'd just started along the path nearest the house when she found him. He drew up short beside a flower-bespeckled hedge, the glow from above cutting shadows into his handsome face. Or maybe it wasn't the moonlight's fault. Perhaps he was truly that grieved.

"Holly?" Chalmys murmured. He stepped closer until he was just out of reach. "Is something wrong? It isn't Violet, is it?"

"She's fine, as far as I know," Holly replied, her heart softening at his concern. She took the stone from her pocket and tapped it. "See? Soundly sleeping. And I'm fine, too, except for some insomnia."

He let out a relieved breath. "That last part I know too well.

Perhaps some soothing tea for both of us? I'm finally tired enough that it might actually work."

Part of her wanted to stay out here in the soft moonlight, with the gentle breeze ruffling Chalmys's robes and surrounding them with the soft scent of flowers she couldn't name. It was so...romantic, dammit. A girl could make foolish decisions standing in the glow of a midnight garden with a kind, attractive man.

Tea, Holly. You can keep your distance over a nice, platonic tea.

"Sure," she said, her voice catching a little on the word. "It's worth a try."

She absolutely ignored the regret she *didn't feel* as he led her back through the house to a too-silent kitchen. Even at night, it seemed like the large room should have been filled with some-thing. A simmering pot atop the stove or pans on a drying rack, maybe. And smells—the scent of spices or freshly baked bread. But if this kitchen had ever been used, every remnant had faded to nothing by now.

Chalmys said not a word as gathered the makings for tea from a cabinet and set them on the long, wooden worktable in the center of the room. Holly hopped onto one of the stools as he filled a kettle with water. Her fingers traced the age-smoothed surface, and she wondered a little about the staff who once would have worked here.

It was too sad a question to ask.

Instead of moving to the stove-looking object halfway down the counter, Chalmys returned to the table with the cold kettle. She lifted a brow in question, and he smiled. "I'll heat it with magic. I long ago ceased renewing the magic on the stove, for I don't enjoy cooking enough to bother with it."

She watched curiously as he sprinkled minty-smelling leaves into a delicate mesh ball and then settled it into the teapot. "That looks like something you'd find in my world."

"For good reason," he said, smiling. "I replicated these tools after I saw them during a scrying session. However, the tea is a blend I grow in the garden. I've come to appreciate it during many sleepless nights."

He held his hand above the kettle, and after a moment, steam rose from the spout. After he'd poured the hot water into the teapot, he claimed the stool beside her. Suddenly, he was far too close, though there was nothing but innocence in the way he sat.

Platonic. Tea.

Holly cleared her throat. "I...hope I didn't upset you earlier."

"By embracing me?" He shook his head. "No, that was nice."

Her cheeks could have set the water in the kettle boiling again. "I didn't mean that. Though I suppose I *should* have asked permission before hugging you."

"On the contrary, you may do so anytime you wish." Chalmys tapped his finger against the table. "Unless I'm doing magic, I suppose. That could be dangerous."

The dim light was both blessing and curse—it would make it harder to notice her blush, but it also made his expression more difficult to read. Was there a greater invitation in his words? Did the man merely long for contact after so long alone? It was impossible to tell, and she was too nervous to ask.

Once again, she cleared her throat. He was going to think she was truly parched. "I, ah, meant... I was worried you were bothered by my questions. I hope I'm not the cause of your sleeplessness. When I saw you from my window, I thought you looked upset."

"Were you looking for me, then?" he asked, his lips curving up slightly.

At the teasing light in his eyes, her heart began to thump a frantic beat. When had this become more dangerous than standing in the moonlight? "I wasn't spying or anything. I just couldn't sleep, and then I looked out the window, and I saw you down there, seeming all sad. Sorry if I intruded. Or caused the problem."

"Do I make you nervous?" Chalmys asked. He poured tea into both their cups, but he made no move to drink his. "It is true that I'm attracted to you, but I would never wish my teasing to make you uncomfortable. I will cease if you wish it."

Holly stared at him, her lips parting in surprise. "I can't believe you just admitted it like that. So easily."

With a shrug, he lifted his cup. "Magic or no, I am but a man, and you are lovely. Beyond even your physical beauty, in fact. I see no reason to pretend otherwise, but I have no expectations of you. Nor did I invite you in here for anything but tea."

"I don't think this tea is very soothing," she blurted.

His grin held more than a little wickedness. "Perhaps you should have a taste before you decide, hmm?"

Oh, God. That *had* to be an innuendo, but one she could easily dismiss if she wasn't interested. He was leaving this up to her. Which was good—except it meant she needed to decide. She might have thought about letting him kiss her earlier, but something in this moment felt...heavier. Maybe momentous.

Her gaze fell to his mouth, and she swallowed hard. In that moment, she knew only one thing for sure—if she left this place without daring even a kiss, she would never forgive herself. She would be shaking her fist about it on her deathbed. So why not? She wasn't going to sleep with him. *At least not tonight,* a traitorous voice whispered before she squashed it. A kiss would be fine.

"Maybe one taste," Holly said softly.

His cup clattered against his saucer, but his hands were gentle when he cupped her face. "You're certain?"

"Yes," she said, covering his hands with her own. "I don't know what it means, but just...just kiss me, Chalmys."

Softly, his lips met hers. One brush. Two. Then, he claimed, and she learned a new kind of magic, one of light and heat and endless tenderness. Her fingers made their way into his hair. One of his hands slid to her neck, his thumb caressing the sensitive skin there. It was absolute perfection captured in one divine moment.

Their lips parted slowly as he pulled away. She couldn't look away from his eyes, dark with passion—a match for the heat spearing through her. She wanted to climb into his lap to be closer to him. Or sit on the worktable in front of him and— *Nope. Bad girl. You will not sleep with a fae mage you've known for less than two weeks.*

Oh, but how she wanted to.

"Thank you," Chalmys said, running his thumb along her lower lip before releasing her entirely. He tossed back his tea like a shot of alcohol and stood. "I hope you rest well, Holly. Thank you for keeping me company tonight."

Then he walked out, leaving her staring after him.

Only later, when she slipped into her too-cold bed, did she realize she'd never learned what had been bothering him.

And that she never had tasted the damn tea.

CHAPTER 20

Chalmys probably shouldn't have kissed Holly, but he couldn't find a single speck of regret for it. In fact, his feet landed lightly against the library floor as he crossed the vast space, and that good humor was in spite of the task he would soon undertake. It had to be the memory of the previous night that bolstered him, a beacon where there would have been only darkness. The heavy weight that had followed him through his nighttime wanderings seemed lessened now.

Beyond the grouping of tables, rows of bookshelves stood sentinel to his interests; unlike the vast shelves lining the walls, the tomes in this section were his most-used. He passed between the shelves without stopping. There was an even more important area concealed behind the decorative panel where he finally halted, a room for storing personal journals and magical texts too dangerous for general use.

With the tap of a crystal, the panel slid open, and he stepped inside. Spells kept away dust and prevented decay, but the rows of ancient books made the space feel musty, anyway. Today, he needed only the large, blue trunk he'd inherited from his mother. He gathered it into a levitation spell and directed it out the door before sealing the panel once more.

There was no need to work in the cramped secret room, after all, not with his only guests here to help him with his quest. He would have to warn Violet not to touch the ancient books, but he didn't doubt that she would comply. Though vibrant and at times excitable, the little girl was overall the responsible sort. She hadn't attempted to enter a single place she'd been told not to go.

He settled the trunk in the empty spot between Holly's working area and a currently unused table. For a moment, he stared down at the soft blue lid covering everything his mother had left to him, and his lightness of spirit dimmed to something more melancholy. Aside from the journals, there wasn't much—a couple of prayer shawls, a decorative fan, a simple gold necklace. So little for a life that had meant so much.

"Chalmys?"

His gaze jumped to the door, where Holly stood with Violet. Both wore confused frowns as they stared at him. "Is it breakfast already?" he asked.

"That's our mission," Holly responded, her eyes narrowing on the trunk. "I really hope that's not holding the other half of your outline."

A surprise laugh burst from his lips. "No. I need to read through my mother's journals to see what I can learn about my father. Will it bother you if I do so here? I thought it might make it easier to share anything relevant."

Holly shook her head. "That's fine. But we're going to eat before I do anything."

However, Violet didn't move when her mother tugged gently on her hand. "Mr. Chalmys, you don't know your father, either? I hope he's not bad like mine."

Something twisted and broke in Chalmys's chest, the peculiar pain unlike anything he'd experienced before. "I know his name, but I have never spoken to him," he replied, his throat nearly strangling the words. He coughed into his hand. "I care not whether he is bad, for my mother raised me well without him."

"Yeah." Violet gave a resolved little nod. "Me, too. Why do you want to know about him, then?"

"Because I want to know if he hurt my mother," Chalmys said. "If he did, he should get in trouble for it."

"Big trouble," the little girl replied. Her firm tone made him wonder if she'd overheard something she shouldn't have the night they'd come here, and Holly's pallor suggested she was worried about the same.

Holly cleared her throat. "What should we have for breakfast today? We should introduce Mr. Chalmys to new Earth food."

Just like that, Violet grinned. "I want to see how many cereals the plate can make!"

The two ladies chatted about their mystery food all the way to the dining room, but Chalmys couldn't focus on it. He was too busy trying to reconstruct his poor, shattered heart. The child had spoken so casually about such a sad issue, one she should never have to deal with at all. Violet deserved a father's love more than her father deserved his miserable life.

Next time, he vowed, *Dylan will not leave my presence unscathed.*

THOUGH HOLLY HAD EXPECTED things to be awkward, somehow breakfast was absolutely normal—aside from magical platters, of course. There was an ease to being here with Chalmys. Was it comfort? Familiarity? She'd always thought it took a long time to build up the latter, but a week in his home had challenged that notion. He simply felt right.

She'd heard of people getting married right after they met. Was this odd sense of belonging what had led them to take that kind of leap? Her hand tightened around her spoon. *Not* that she was considering marrying the guy because of a pleasant post-kiss breakfast. No relationship, either. Or sex.

Nothing but work to do here.

Holly sighed, her breath rippling the milk in her bowl and sending the little circles of cereal bobbling. Leave it to her to find the perfect man...who also happened to be a cursed fae mage from another dimension. Even if she helped to free him, they lived in different worlds. He would have no use for Earth, and beyond her own wishes, she had a child to consider. Even if Holly decided she liked this fantasy realm, Violet might not. And there was school, family—

"Did the platter not deliver accurate cereal?" Chalmys asked. "You appear to be scowling at it mightily."

Grimacing, she shook her head. "No, sorry. It's fine. I just have a lot to think about."

His forehead wrinkled. "If last night—"

"No, no," Holly interrupted, tipping her head slightly toward Violet. "Our *discussion* last night was great. Please don't worry about that. I was actually wondering what you might do after you're free."

Well, it was sort of true.

"Honestly, I'm not sure," Chalmys said. "I imagine I would explore a bit. Check on old friends Perhaps see some of the wonders on Earth for myself."

Violet glanced up from her cereal. "You'd leave your magic house? But it's perfect here!"

A slight smile crossed Chalmys's lips as he looked fondly at her daughter. "I doubt I would stay gone for long. After so long, I'm rather accustomed to being here."

"You need a magic closet," Violet mused. "Or a door. Then you could walk through and *poof!* Earth. I'd want one to go see Gram and Papa and my uncles. Gram says it's about time Uncle Max gets married, so maybe I'll have cousins to play with soon. Can't miss that."

Holly chuckled. "Slow down, sweetie. Your uncle probably needs to meet the right girl first. Or any girl. That's what Gram meant."

Though she was curious to hear more of Chalmys's plans,

Holly let the conversation drift to a discussion about her brother and his work. There was a danger in asking too much about the mage's intentions, especially in front of her daughter. The more she and Violet learned, the more there was for them to accidentally hook their errant hopes upon.

Eventually, they returned to the library, each with their own tasks in mind. Violet was staging a coup against the Queen of Ice Cream in favor of Empress Chocolate Cake—no doubt what her daughter would want for dessert—and Chalmys had started sorting through the chest between their tables. Holly did her best to focus on her notes and not the muscles that worked in his back every time he leaned over for more books.

At least he was sitting, or it would be another piece of his anatomy constantly in her line-of-sight. Talk about a distraction. Really, how did a mage have such a firm ass? Shouldn't he be too busy doing magic stuff to exercise that much? Maybe it was a natural part of being fae. They *were* generally described as beautiful.

"Maaaamaaaaa."

Holly's gaze snapped to Violet, who was currently tugging on her sleeve. "I'm sorry, Vi. What's wrong?"

"Nothing, except you weren't answering." Her daughter frowned at Chalmys. "Is there something on Mr. Chalmys's back? You were staring so hard at it."

The man in question startled at that, his side connecting with the corner of the table with enough force to shake the books spread out atop it. Holly cupped her hand against her burning face to block him from her sight. If she couldn't see him, he couldn't see her, right? *Too bad baby logic doesn't work when you need it to.*

"Did you want to go outside, sweetie?" Holly asked, her voice a little too high-pitched.

Please let that other question go.

Violet's frown shifted into something a little more calculating, but her eventual smile was sweet enough. "Not right now. I was just wondering how fairies learn. Is there a school somewhere on this world? I could enjoy learning with fairies."

Ohhhh no. There was that hope looking for a nice place to hook.

"Fae," Chalmys said as he straightened, rubbing at the spot on his side. "If you're asking about my people, we're called fae. There are schools for our children, of course, but many learn at home with private tutors. That's doubly likely if the child has a strong talent for magic, since that can manifest in so many ways. Individual attention is best in that case."

Violet blinked at him, and Holly laughed. "Yes, there are schools, but a lot of kids are homeschooled. Especially if they have strong magic," she translated.

"I got most of it," her daughter said. Then she whispered, "Man-uh-fessst" like she was memorizing some arcane chant.

With a grin, Chalmys strode over to one of the tall bookcases lining the wall beside them. His head tilted adorably as he read the spines, enough that she almost hated to see him pull a couple of thin volumes out. He brought the small, leather-bound books over and set them on the table in front of Violet.

"If you're wanting to learn like a child here, you could study these." He tapped his finger on the top book. "They're for teaching fae children to read. You'll not understand what any of our words mean, of course, but if you run your finger over the letters inside this book, you'll hear what the symbols are supposed to sound like. The second book *will* teach you a few words, but I'm afraid they are very simple ones. These are for children a couple of years younger than you."

Holly lifted a brow. Why did a single man have reading primers in his library?

Catching her glance, his cheeks reddened slightly. "When I first started this collection, I'd still thought to have a family of my own. I also have books on pregnancy, childbirth, child development—"

"Okay, okay," Holly interrupted, uncomfortable with the

warmth sliding through her at his sweetness. "You really don't have to explain."

Damn, though. The god who'd cursed him to this kind of loneliness was a real asshole.

And hopefully not omniscient.

Violet opened the top book and touched the first symbol, which released an "eh" sound. Her daughter grinned and clapped. "It's an E."

"Ah, not quite," Chalmys corrected gently. "These don't match up with your letters exactly. There's another one for the 'ee' sound. Come, I'll show you while your mother works."

Before Holly knew it, Violet had settled a few tables down with Chalmys. They hunched together over the book, her daughter touching letters and the mage giving his explanations in a low, gentle voice. Good grief. The man was voluntarily teaching her daughter how to read another language, and Holly was supposed to do something besides watch them? It was just too cute to resist.

The thought made her freeze.

Oh, no. I might already have some of that hope, too.

Her and Chalmys. That would be impossible, wouldn't it? Absolutely. But the ache in her chest wasn't pain—it was too heady for that. It lingered even as she continued her notes on his life, each noble deed confirmed by a glance at the man working so patiently with her daughter. He might have been a battle mage, but he was inherently kind.

Reassuring, but far too much trouble for her heart.

ONCE AGAIN, Chalmys felt a sense of lightness as he returned to his table. The decision to show Violet a little about his language had been spontaneous, so he'd been surprised by how much interest she took in it. She'd already learned the words for book, library, mother, father, tree, dragon, and—of course—unicorn. Verbally, at least. She hadn't mastered the letters yet.

"She wasn't too much trouble, was she?" Holly asked softly as Violet darted out the door, intent on exploring the garden.

"Of course not," Chalmys answered. "She is well-behaved and quite clever."

Holly smiled. "That doesn't mean she doesn't have her moments. Like when I tried to get her to eat more broccoli the other night."

Ah, yes. It had been the first time he'd seen the little girl sulk and argue to such an extent. He grinned. "Books *are* better than broccoli."

"Not for eating," Holly quipped.

In this situation, they were both correct.

Still smiling, Chalmys lifted the first journal from the pile. He ran his finger over the worn, cream-colored cover and recalled how his mother had leaned over her desk to write in her little books. Last time, the memory had filled him with sadness, but it was a bittersweet ache now. She'd been as religious about her nightly accounts as she'd been about her prayers.

He opened the book, and his heart caught upon the fine loops and curls of her handwriting. He'd spent centuries reading notes and letters written by her hand. As he stared down at the first page, the years since her death disappeared. Her spirit was there as it had always been. If the thought of that hadn't pained him so greatly over the centuries, he might have found the secrets within these pages sooner.

If there were any.

It was slow-going. Though she'd written something nearly every day, some entries were only a couple of lines. Some filled multiple pages. Her early life at the temple. Her training. How she'd felt about making her formal vows. Most of it was straightforward, but it still took time to skim through since he couldn't say for sure when she'd first met his father.

Chalmys was reading about her second assignment at a countess's estate when Holly slipped out to get Violet luncheon, and he'd barely moved on to his mother's return to the main temple complex when the two of them came back. Still no mention of Kleress. How often had his mother gone to work as a priestess at noble estates? She hadn't done so in his memory, but in these accounts, she seemed to have enjoyed it.

With a sharp clack, Holly set a plate beside his elbow. "You need to eat something. You can't research anything if you starve."

"Empress Chococake can help," Violet called from her table of unicorns.

Though he smiled, he thought it best not to ask about the odd-sounding "chococake." He would rather focus on the small, hearty loaf of bread and slices of meat Holly had brought. "I'd intended to wait until I was done reading for the day before I ate. With these books being so old..."

"So sit over there," Holly said, hitching her thumb toward the table behind her.

Her logic was impeccable.

He placed a page marker in his current book and sighed to note that it was only the second out of over a hundred journals. "I suppose I might as well. This will be no quick task."

As he shifted tables, Holly frowned down at the little books. "Too bad I can't help. I haven't even learned as much of your language as Violet has."

It was a problem he'd encountered often, too. Holding his bread with one hand, he lifted the other and summoned the eyepiece from his desk into his palm. Like the loupe he'd created to examine jewelry, this little silver V affixed to the nose. But it had a different purpose. It translated words into the wearer's language.

He held the device up. "This will let you read it."

"Really?" Her wide eyes met his. "Then why the primers for Violet?"

Chalmys shrugged. "It doesn't teach you the words, though with enough effort, the device can help alongside regular studies."

She appeared to consider that a moment before nodding.

"Okay, then. If it doesn't bother you, I would be happy to help when you return to the task. I have a feeling this is far more important than what I'm doing."

He suspected that she was correct, but normally, he never would have considered accepting her aid. Not when it meant letting a human—even one with latent fae blood—read the journal of a fae priestess who also happened to be his mother. Holly, though? He knew without a doubt that he could trust her.

Nodding, Chalmys settled the device into her hand.

CHAPTER 21

After several days of reading, Holly's nose ached from wearing the translation device, but she didn't mind. Reading about his mother's life was beyond fascinating. Not just because the journals told a great deal about this world and its religion but because of Lady Larah's insights. It was clear by her words that she'd enjoyed being a priestess, especially the way she'd contemplated the meaning behind temperance at length.

Balance, Larah had said, *Remains the fundamental struggle, an equilibrium that requires sometimes-contradictory movements to maintain.*

"Your mother was quite the philosopher," Holly said.

Chalmys glanced up from the journal he was reading. "That is true. I've never met another priestess as deserving of a final reward as my mother. It eats at me that my life might cause her to lose it."

"I'm sorry." Holly squeezed his forearm. "If we don't find what that god of yours suspects, then I'll do my best to get around mentioning her in your story. Clever wording can go a long way."

He lifted her hand to his lips, and the soft kiss sent a tingle up her arm. "Thank you."

It took a great deal of willpower to return to work, but there was an urgency building inside that she couldn't deny. In theory, it was because of her own limited time here. Summer only lasted a couple of months, after all. And yet... Chalmys had mentioned that his father would become the official crown prince soon and that the god Vier had been worried about that. The fact had settled into her head and refused to leave.

So she read and read until her eyes grew tired from it. Eventually, even novelty and fascination faded away until it felt more like one of her freelance jobs. Skim. Make notes. Repeat. But if it helped him, it would be worthwhile.

"Hmm."

At the noise from Chalmys, she glanced over. "Find something?"

"My father came to the temple to request a priestess to serve in his private chapel. According to my mother, the high priestess was upset for days." Chalmys's forehead furrowed. "This was a couple of centuries before I was born."

Holly switched to reading journals closer in time to that one. Over and over, they ran across the same thing. Priestesses were requested, only to return within a handful of years. They were never truly the same, either. More solemn and reserved. Sometimes fearful. Another few years might pass when the prince drew priestesses from other gods' temples, but then the cycle would repeat.

"I don't want to jump to conclusions..." Holly began.

She didn't have to finish. "He must have coerced them," Chalmys said solemnly.

"But Chalmys." She pointed at the entry she was reading. "Right here, your mother wrote her suspicions about it all. So why would she have gone? Were they chosen randomly?"

For a moment, he didn't answer, his eyes locked on the page. "No. She volunteered. See?"

Holly read over his shoulder. *Balance must clearly be restored. If a greater motion is needed to return the prince to order, then I shall be the one to deliver it. It is beyond my comprehension that the high priestess has sent such young ones in the past, but it will be the case no longer.*

Lady Larah had gone on purpose. And an uneasy whisper suggested that the priestess's fierce intentions had gone terribly awry.

CHALMYS HAD SPENT decades of his life in war zones, fighting against rogue mages and devious tyrants. He'd tracked cunning wizards through forest mazes and delivered justice to more than one oppressor. Once, he'd carried a duchess to safety while her severed foot leaked a trail of blood. The prince who'd captured her had nearly found them by matching the trail with the blood left in her shoe.

None of it had been worse than reading this.

I am certain his kindness is a lie, for well I can read the dark intentions lurking in his eyes when he looks at me. In truth, he mocks me. Even as I perform rituals, his gaze follows me as though I am the weakest of prey. I understand the heat there perfectly. I was no virgin before taking my oaths to remain chaste.

Although Chalmys had been raised at the temple, he hadn't realized such a thing was allowed. Yet another sign of how little he'd known of his mother and her life. With shaking fingers, he kept turning the pages, his heart breaking more with each entry.

I cannot stop this, but I can see it. He doesn't know. He believes me entirely subsumed by his power, yet part of my mind will not yield. I don't know what to do. Thrice he has claimed my body during the New Moon rituals—and only then. He murmurs of Iperan, whose High Rituals occur at that time. But Kleress only has a quarter of Iperan's blood. What right has he to do this? Most of all, why doesn't the goddess intercede? I do not know.

Bile rose up Chalmys's throat, horror almost blocking out reason. But his mother's question repeated endlessly through his mind. Why hadn't the goddess interceded? If the prince had done this in the middle of a ceremony, Peorban had surely noticed. Why require a vow, only to remain silent when it was forcibly broken?

It cannot go unnoticed that I am with child. In a panic, I wrote a letter of confession to the high priestess. Her only response? Let Kleress take care of everything. This can't be the first time, then. Why, why, why? All I can think of is the balance. Is this the unexpected motion that evens out the weight of too much chastity? Will I pay with my soul?

Yet I cannot regret it. The child stirs within me, and my heart sings. I'm alone now, only a single servant here to attend to me, but I do not feel lonely. My spirit cries that this child is my balance—and perhaps the same for others someday. The goddess Peorban must want my baby born, for I continue my formal rituals to Her even in isolation. She must see him.

May She also bless him.

Chalmys closed the book over the page marker with a thud. The tension sapped from his muscles, his head hanging low as the implications thundered in his mind. He'd been conceived in the middle of a ritual, but not one that allowed for sex. The goddess should have known, yet he'd been a dark secret, anyway. Like his mother, his mind struggled repeatedly over the *why*.

Holly rubbed soothing circles on his back. "I'm guessing it's bad."

He couldn't lift his head. "My...father...coerced her during rituals. Sacred ceremonies, in fact. Vier was correct. I'm living proof of Kleress's blasphemies."

Did he deserve this curse, then? No matter Vier's protestations, he must have thought Chalmys's existence appalling, and that was without knowing the full details of his conception. Anyone who heard of this would be horrified. Being a descendant of Iperan, God of Metalworking, would have given Kleress no right.

Suddenly, Holly's fingers dug into his shoulder, and she gave him a hard shake. "Stop it. Do you think you're tainted somehow?" She shoved a crystal in front of his eyes, filling his vision with Violet's smiling face. "Maybe there weren't rituals involved, but her father used me, then ditched us when I got pregnant. He's a greedy, amoral fuck who would've killed me for money. Do you want to go out there and tell Violet that *she's* tainted?"

The image faded from the crystal, but it played in his inner sight. "Of course not. But mundane—"

Holly shook him again. "Evil doesn't give a crap where it happens, Chalmys. Whether you're at a temple or walking down the street, it does its harm all the same. You, your mother...you're both victims. That is all."

He shifted around in his seat, the motion forcing her hand to slip from his shoulder. The indignation in her eyes relaxed some knot of despair deep inside him, and he knew without question that she was upset *for* him.

"I feel terrible," he murmured.

"Of course you do." Holly brushed her knuckle gently across his cheek. "But it really isn't your fault. I promise."

Chalmys turned his head, pressing a kiss to her finger before she withdrew her hand. Her little shiver brought him his first hint of peace since opening the journal. "I need to think about this. And yet *not* think. It's maddening."

Holly seemed to understand.

"There's dinner still to get through." She nudged her knee against his, and a little smile tipped her lips. "Violet plans to coax you into trying chocolate cake. She said the empress is very disappointed, and as unicorns are stabby creatures, I suspect you won't want to risk her ire."

Despite the dark worry lingering in his heart, Chalmys chuckled. The first time Violet had summoned the odd cake, he'd refused to try it. Though it smelled fine enough, it had the color of newly turned soil covered in fresh mud. But he *did* need a distraction.

Since Holly had yet to initiate another kiss, he supposed the suspiciously brown cake would have to do.

HOLLY HAD JUST enough time to read those terrible journal entries before Violet ran in demanding cake, and that sudden influx of cheer had stabbed at her like a knife. Innocence and joy made a bitter counterpoint to the sad tale of abuse—and all the more because of the similarities between their stories. No, Holly hadn't been tricked into sex with magic. Otherwise, though? Chalmys and Violet were both so good at heart despite their terrible fathers. No wonder they got along so well.

Chalmys boosted Violet onto his shoulders, her happy chatter accompanying them all the way to the dining room. Holly knew he was in emotional pain, but he hid it well. She noticed it in the flattened curve of his smile and the small, spare bites he took of the soup he summoned. His laughter didn't ring as true, either. But all of those cues were too slight for her daughter to notice.

He even relented on the cake. She grinned at the sight, for only when the chocolate hit his tongue did his feigned pleasure shift to something true. "We told you it wasn't dirt."

Chalmys lifted a brow. "Surely, you can't blame me for the comparison."

"Fine," Holly said, eyeing the color. "I guess not."

He retreated to his workroom after dinner. But later, after she'd helped Violet with her bath and tucked her into bed, Holly couldn't find him anywhere. No answer when she tapped the crystal beside the workroom door. No sign of him in the library or on any of the garden paths. Had he gone to bed? She'd wanted to be sure he was okay.

At the base of the stairs, Holly closed her eyes. Much as she'd started sensing him at her home, she could sometimes detect when Chalmys was nearby. She wasn't sure if it was his magic or some kind of aura, but she just *knew*. Could she stretch that sense a bit? She visualized herself walking through the house and did her best to feel for his energy.

When they connected mentally, she yelped in surprise.

"Holly?"

"I was trying to figure out where you were," she hurried to say —think—whatever. *"Can you hear this?"*

A hint of warmth brushed against her mind. *"Yes. I'd thought to go to bed early, but I've done nothing but stare at the ceiling. I fear it will be a long night."*

"This probably doesn't help," she replied, wincing.

"Don't worry about it. I'll be fine, but I thank you for your concern," he said. Aloud, his words might have been convincing, but the strange mental link allowed his sorrow to seep through. *"I hope you'll fare better at sleep."*

Gently, Chalmys severed the link, and she found herself staring at the wall beside the stairs. Not for long, though. She made her way to the kitchen where they'd shared their first spectacular kiss. As usual, it rang with a sad, abandoned feel, but she'd grown used to it. She made tea often here now, since Chalmys had enchanted the kettle for her. He'd even labeled the little containers of tea leaves lined up on the work table.

He was sad, lonely, hurting, and now unable to sleep it all away. She might not be able to change his past, nor could she ease the ache of the day's discovery. But she could make him a pot of tea. Maybe see if he needed to talk about it all before he could rest. He'd done so much to help her. It seemed a small thing to offer a cup of tea in return.

Porcelain rattled against silver as she carried the tray up the stairs and down the hall to his door. There, she hesitated. How was she supposed to knock? She wasn't adept enough at balancing tea sets to hold the surprisingly heavy tray steady with one hand. Maybe she should kick the door. It would make a louder, ruder sound, but it would get his attention.

The door opened before she could decide.

Holly nearly dropped the tray. He wore nothing but a pair of thin pants, so low-slung that his hip bones appeared to balance their weight. Damn. He was indeed muscular, though not overly so. Just enough to create lines she'd love to trace with her tongue.

Right down to those hip bones, and...that wasn't the only thing holding his pants up now.

"Holly." His hands covered hers. "Holly, the tray."

She had to jerk her gaze up, away from the greatest temptation she'd ever seen in her life—though the wicked invitation in his eyes came in a close second. "Crap. Sorry. I should have thought you'd be naked. I mean, not *naked* naked. Just...I should probably leave the tea and go."

He didn't move his hands. "You needn't. I can grab a shirt if it'll make you more comfortable."

"No!" Holly blurted. Too loudly, of course. But who wanted to cover a masterpiece? "Don't worry about it. We're both adults."

Oh, yeah. There was definitely wickedness in that gaze. But he nodded and released her hands. "Come in. If you're having trouble sleeping, perhaps we can both have a cup."

She couldn't help looking at his lips. Last time they'd shared this tea, they had ended up kissing. Why hadn't she thought of that before coming up with this plan? *You're supposed to be comforting him, Holly. Not ogling him.* With that reminder, she nodded and moved past him into the room.

At the end of their initial tour, he'd finally shown them his room, though only from the doorway. It was far more beautiful once inside. Though her room was lovely, it was somewhat impersonal. This chamber absolutely spoke of him, with its warm wood and jewel-toned fabrics. She placed the tray on the small dining table beside a gorgeous geode full of bright blue crystals. She would just bet that he'd found that geode himself.

Chalmys slipped up beside her, his shoulder brushing hers. "Thank you for thinking of me."

She turned to face him, and their gazes locked. "Sometimes, I can't think of much else," she blurted.

Oh, God. She couldn't stand this. Could. Not.

She wrapped her arms around his waist and leaned up to kiss him.

CHAPTER 22

It only took a second for Chalmys's hands to catch up with his heart.

Gently, he cupped the back of Holly's head in his palms, his fingers tangling in her hair as he devoured her sweetly offered mouth. She tasted of chocolate cake and ambrosia. An elixir he needed to live. Ah, it felt like forever since their last kiss. Eternity without her mouth upon his and her body tucked close.

He didn't want to think about when she left.

Desperation lent an edge to his kiss. He had to force himself to pull back before he lost all control, for he would never risk hurting or scaring her. One last time, he sucked on her lower lip, easing the pinch with a swipe of his tongue. Then he rested his forehead against hers. For a moment, their panting breaths clashed in the space between their lips.

"Why did you stop?" Holly whispered.

Chalmys glided one hand down her back until it rested low on her waist. Then he pulled her tight against him until she couldn't mistake the extent of his desire. "My hold on my control... If I kiss you too long now, I'll want to have all of you. All night."

Forever, but that was impossible.

She tipped her head back, her gaze boring into his with unexpected intensity. "You didn't ask my thoughts on the matter."

She wiggled against him, and his breath caught. "And they are?"

"I want you, too." Her fingers dug into his back. "Badly. But you haven't made another move, so—"

He claimed her lips once more.

She moaned against his mouth, and as he slipped his fingers beneath the waistband of her little shorts, she wrapped one of her legs around his waist. This time, he was the one who let out a low, helpless moan. He had to have her. Frenzied, he spun her around, lifting until her bottom rested on the table.

At the rattle of porcelain, Chalmys wrapped a levitation spell around the tray and resettled it atop his desk with a decided crash. Holly gave a tiny, breathless chuckle. "There's a perfectly nice bed over there. And the geode..."

He sent the thing to the floor with the same general finesse as the tea set. It didn't matter. He wouldn't waste this night with her on trivialities, not when he might never have another. So he pulled the thin sleeping shirt over her head and tossed it somewhere behind him. Only then did he slow—for her pleasure wasn't trivial at all.

◆

HOLLY WASN'T sure how she'd ended up boneless atop a table with Chalmys kissing his way up her body, but it had to be some kind of divine intervention. Though he hadn't entered her yet, he'd already claimed her rather thoroughly. She hadn't expected a man who'd lived alone for centuries to have such a clever tongue.

Which he demonstrated again with her nipple. Damn.

"Unngh," she managed when his hard length slid over her clit.

He only chuckled against her breast. "May I make you mine, dearest one?"

Didn't he know she already was? "Now. Quickly."

"Ah, but not like this." He pulled back a little, and she began contemplating how one might kill a powerful fae mage. The torturer. Grinning, he nipped at her lower lip. "I don't want to hurt you."

Chalmys scooped her against him and then straightened, one arm under her butt and the other cradling her back as though he carried treasure. Planning a murder might have been premature, although the torment was real as he strode across the room. With each step, her sensitive body brushed against his until she wanted to scream.

Soft sheets welcomed her as he lowered her to his bed, but still, he didn't enter her. "Chalmys, if you don't..."

His tongue traced a line up her stomach, arresting all thought.

Her world became sensation. His skin against hers. Soft caresses and heated kisses. She sank into it. Reveled in it. When finally he took her, there was nothing but him. Them. Her nails dug into his back almost fiercely as he began to move.

Mine, she wanted to shout.

Unfortunately, she couldn't. So she rose to meet him, claiming him in her own way as they brought each other to pleasure. And in that perfect, final moment, she almost felt she could touch his soul.

HOLLY SHIFTED AGAINST CHALMYS, her arm tightening around his waist as she snuggled closer. Damn, her body ached—but in a good way. This kind of sore was a blessing she hadn't received in far too long. Really, though, she should have guessed he would be a generous lover. Her only real regret was that she hadn't jumped him in the kitchen the night of their first kiss.

Wasted time.

"If I weren't a captive, I would court you," Chalmys murmured.

Her heart picked up its beat, and she leaned back so she could see his face. He wore a soft, sad expression that made her want to kiss him. "What does that matter?" she asked. "I'm here now, aren't I?"

His brows drew together. "I will not trap you and Violet in my torment. It would be selfish."

Although Holly didn't precisely *want* to be stuck here by a curse, she felt like the man could use a little selfishness. It was undeniably noble to protect his mother, but as a mother herself, she had to wonder if Lady Larah wept in the afterlife over his sacrifice. Holly wouldn't want Violet to be miserable on her behalf, no matter the cost. But Chalmys wasn't the type to yield on such an important cause.

"I suppose I'll have to free you," she replied. Her gaze slipped to his lips. "Then...we'll see. I don't know what to make of this or how any of it would work. But..."

But he really did feel like hers now. She couldn't explain it, yet it was true.

Not that she could say that without sounding crazy.

Chalmys smiled down at her. "I'll have to return to my outline with greater verve."

"Yeah." His fingers trailed down her side, and her body went hot all over again. "Tomorrow, though. We have a bit of time before I need to return to my room."

And she was going to make the most of it.

CHALMYS WOKE the moment the hand landed on the doorknob. His eyelids snapped open, his arm curling Holly protectively close as he scanned. Only to immediately relax. It was Violet. With a wave of his hand, he summoned their discarded clothes to them, ensuring they were dressed before the child entered. Though Holly shifted against him at the slide of fabric, she didn't wake.

The door opened a crack. "Mr. Chalmys? I need help."

He smiled at her sweet, tentative voice. She must be looking for her mother. "You may come in," he said.

Slowly, the crack widened until the little girl could ease through. Her forehead was wrinkled with worry, but her gaze darted around nervously as she finally stepped inside. "Are you sure? You have to have a lot of magic in here. Oh, your rock fell on the ground. But I promise I won't pick it up, even though it's pretty."

"Nothing in here will harm you," he said, though he made note to put a warning shield a little farther from his door. His combat instincts had dulled over the centuries here, but they weren't gone. "How may I help you, young Violet?"

"There was light in the window, so I went to find Mama because I'm hungry, but she wasn't in her bed. And I was going to look around some, but it's shadowy, and there are places I'm not supposed to go, and I remembered I should get a grown-up's help," the child said in one long rush.

Holly stirred at the sound of her daughter's voice, drawing the child's attention. "Mmm. Violet?" She blinked her eyes open, then froze. "Chalmys."

Violet's mouth dropped open on a gasp. "Mama! I knew it. I *knew* Mr. Chalmys was going to be my new dad."

A surge of happiness flashed through him at the thought, but he couldn't let the child form the wrong impression. "Though such a thing would be an honor, I'm afraid I haven't had the pleasure of marrying your mother."

The mother in question buried her reddened face against his chest and groaned.

Violet, on the other hand, was undaunted. "I don't care about that. You're sharing a room together like parents do. Jaynie said her mom and dad sleep in the same bed. And Bryson's moms. Everyone with two parents said that's what happens."

Nothing in any world could have stopped Chalmys's grin. "Is that so?"

"Yeah," the little girl said. Then her face scrunched up.

"Except I sleep in Mama's bed sometimes, and I'm not my own mom. That would be weird."

Holly's head darted up, her sigh warming the fabric of his shirt. "Violet. Sweetie. Anyone can nap together without being married. Or even in a relationship. I...fell asleep here after comforting Mr. Chalmys. He did *not* sign up for parenthood."

The child's face fell, and in that moment, he wanted nothing more than to tell her he would love to be her father. To love, guide, and protect her. But it was a vow he didn't have the right to make, especially not with things so uncertain with Holly. It would be cruel to make a promise he wasn't sure he could keep.

"I'm honored by your assumption," Chalmys said carefully. "But I wouldn't dare to propose marriage to your mother in my current situation. For one thing, it would be difficult to make that door you suggested. You'll want to visit your Earth family with ease, correct?"

Holly went still beside him as Violet puzzled that over. "Can't you just man-you-fest it?"

It took him a moment to translate that one. "I can only partly manifest it right now. For safety, I would need to cross to Earth to anchor it, and I'm unable to do that."

"Oh." Hurt had been replaced by a speculative gleam in her eyes. "So Mama needs to work on your story more. Okay. I'm gonna go get dressed, Mama, okay?"

"Sure. I'll come get you for breakfast in a minute," Holly said.

As soon as the door closed behind Violet, Holly flopped onto her back, her arm covering her eyes. "Kids say the darndest things," she muttered.

Was she angry?

Chalmys propped himself up on his elbow. He longed to settle his hand on her waist—maybe kiss her—but now, he was uncertain of his reception. She'd seemed to be considering a relationship the night before. Had he misunderstood? Hurt twisted in his chest, though he had no right to feel it. She owed him nothing, after all.

"I'm sorry," he said. "I hope my response wasn't inappropriate or presumptuous."

She peeked at him from beneath her arm. "Why are *you* sorry? It's my child who keeps jumping to conclusions and making things awkward for you."

He lifted a strand of her hair and flicked it against his lips. "I don't feel awkward. I feel only longing. Didn't I say I would court you if I weren't trapped? That means acceptance of Violet, too."

"Oh." Holly's throat worked. "I'm afraid that isn't usually my dating experience."

Chalmys shrugged. "And this isn't your usual world."

He dropped her hair, and her gaze followed the motion. Then she frowned. "Umm. Did I seriously get up to put my clothes on, then hop back in bed? Why didn't I go back to my room?"

"I summoned our clothes to us when I sensed Violet at the door. Magic can solve many unexpected dilemmas." He grinned at her wide-eyed expression. "Come back tonight, and I'll be happy to show you more."

With a light laugh, she shoved him to his back, but instead of pouncing, she leaped from the bed. "Maybe. But I don't know if I should bring tea this time. I haven't decided if the stuff is cursed or blessed, but either way, I still don't know what it tastes like."

His grin widened. He couldn't deny being pleased at creating such a distraction.

CHAPTER 23

*H*olly frowned down at her latest page of notes, though she should have been happy. She was almost done working through the first half of the outline, and after what they'd found in his mother's journals, she felt confident she could write a solid story of Chalmys's life as soon as she had the rest of his outline. It was just that...working in the library without him was lonely.

Especially since Violet had abandoned both unicorn toys and reading primers for her daily adventure in the play garden. Of course, that adventure would surely be longer, since a certain mage had created an entire child-sized castle tower—complete with a moat and enough safety spells to satisfy the most cautious parent alive—after Violet had gone to bed last night.

He would probably do something that elaborate again, too, since Holly had rewarded him thoroughly when they'd returned to his room. But dammit, his pride and excitement over the surprise had been hotter than she ever would have expected. So weak. She was so weak when he did something that adorable.

Ugh. Why had he decided to complete the outline in his workroom? Sure, Violet had nearly caught them kissing once, but *only* once. They could've worked like adults instead of getting distracted. Like now. She was working, not... Okay, she was thinking of him instead of the task at hand.

No wonder Chalmys was in the other room.

She really needed to focus. The sooner she could tell his story, the sooner he would be free. Then she could find out what form "courting" would take from the man she'd already spent the last three nights with. Honestly, she wasn't sure he could improve on his methods, because the amount of care he put into his every action already wrecked her.

So. Note-taking.

By the time Chalmys reappeared, the light from the windows stretched long across the floor. "I'm finished with the outline," he said, waving a stack of papers. "And I have a note from your brother, too. It was there when I sent your letter."

Holly grabbed both with equal eagerness, though she left the rest of Chalmys's outline on the table in favor of the note. The paper felt too thin and slick against her fingers after dealing with so much parchment, but Max's handwriting was a comfort. The message...not so much. With each word she read, her stomach clenched tighter.

"What's wrong?" Chalmys asked, easing closer to her chair.

"Dylan did show up at my brother's house," she replied. The paper shook in her hand. "Max said he hadn't seen us. Then Dylan started ranting about government experiments, weird drugs, and witches, and he wouldn't go away even after Max went inside. Soooo, now my ex is in jail because he started waving a gun out on the sidewalk. And for possession of drugs, because of course he had those *and* a gun. God, Chalmys. How did he turn so bad? He wasn't great in college, but damn."

Chalmys massaged the back of her neck with gentle fingers. "He let you and Violet go, so his decision-making skills were clearly lacking even in his youth. But...arrested. What will that mean for you and your family, exactly?"

"I don't know." Holly let her eyes slip closed, the comfort of Chalmys's touch easing some of her worry. "He'll probably go to prison, but I've never paid that much attention to that kind of stuff. I guess it depends on the laws in my brother's area. If nothing else, though, Dylan won't be able to bother us for a while."

He really, really wouldn't.

There was no way Max would refuse to press charges, if that was an option, but even without that, she was pretty sure Dylan had committed a felony. That meant a year or two in prison, surely. If not, her brother would be watching the case closely enough to give her fair warning. Her stomach muscles unclenched, and she sagged in Chalmys's hold. She wouldn't have to fear being at her own house anymore. She had breathing room.

Except...she wasn't sure she wanted to return there now. Could she and Violet find a way to stay? *Hah. You can't think about that until you manage to free Chalmys.* The question would be moot if her story wasn't good enough, since he wasn't allowed to have visitors for long. Now, though, she would at least be able to think about it without worrying about Dylan. That was something.

All she needed to do was write a story, right?

"So," she said, straightening. "Let me have a look at the rest of this outline. Maybe we can *both* get rid of our burdens."

With her resolve strengthened, not even Chalmys could distract her.

AFTER DINNER, Chalmys accompanied Violet to the garden while her mother returned to work. Twilight gilded the trees and gave the new tower a magical glow—perfect framing for the little girl standing at the top. She tossed flowers over the side, and the spell he'd placed caught the petals and carried them gently to the ground, just like anything else that might fall. Violet loved it. Petal after petal drifted onto the rocks she'd tossed over earlier.

He'd glimpsed her playing earlier on his way back from the

stone circle, but now he kept a firmer eye on her. It was almost night, and while he'd warded his gardens against nearly any danger, there was no spell to prevent slipping in the dark. Perhaps he should consider increasing the light globes in the area. There would still be deeper shadows, but it would increase safety somewhat. Especially around the ill-conceived moat. Though it was only ankle deep, he'd regretted creating it almost immediately.

"Look, Mr. Chalmys," Violet called, finally throwing another rock over the edge.

It drifted down as softly as the flower.

"I told you that you could drop the 'mister,'" he reminded her.

She shrugged. "I can't remember. I think 'dad' would be way easier."

The child had become such a champion of unsubtle hints that Holly didn't even blush over them anymore. Chalmys merely chuckled. "So you have said."

He waited until it was fully dark to call her down.

Violet had just crossed the tiny bridge over the moat when the summons rang through him. He stiffened, the smile dropping from his face. Vier called for him again? Why? Chalmys ground his teeth together and gestured for Violet to come with him. The god would have to wait until he had her safely inside with her mother.

On the path, the child grabbed his hand. "What was that ringing sound?"

He missed a step, nearly falling as he'd worried she might do. "You heard it?"

"Yeah." Her little voice wavered. "Is that bad?"

"No." Which was probably true, Vier not being one to harm children. "Only surprising, since it's done that before. Did you hear it then?"

Violet shook her head no, but that was more worrisome than the opposite. That meant she'd been intended to hear, and he could think of no good reason for that. Never in all his centuries here had Chalmys seen a guest be summoned. Had Vier decided to interfere for his own selfish whims?

They'd barely slipped through the back door when Holly rushed over. "What's going on? I heard a weird bell. Or maybe a gong?"

Chalmys used the most arcane language he knew for the string of curses he muttered. No, this couldn't be good. "I'm not sure why, but it seems Vier has summoned us. All of us, in fact."

And if the god messed with Holly or Violet, he would know Chalmys's wrath.

* * *

HOLLY NIBBLED on her lip as they entered the workroom. Chalmys had grown so expressive around her that the contained anger blanking his expression made her skin prickle far more than the bell had. Maybe even more than the summons itself. Still, he touched her as usual, like the hand he rested on her lower back when they stopped on the far side of the room.

This anger wasn't for her.

"I'm scared," Violet whispered. "Is God mad at me?"

Chalmys crouched down beside her, the tight lines softening on his face. "Don't worry, little love. Vier is only one of many gods on this world, but I promise I will protect you from all of them."

Violet grabbed one of his fingers. "Can you carry me?"

"Certainly," he said. "I'm going to cast a magic shield around us, so don't be alarmed."

As Chalmys lifted her daughter, settling her on his hip, Holly's heart melted. There was simply no other way to describe it. Her heart just squeezed itself into a mushy lump and then melted until all she could feel was warmth spreading through her whole body. She loved him. This kind but fierce man who held her daughter with one hand and did some magic spell with the other—she loved him. And if some cruel god thought he could separate them, well... She wasn't sure what she would do, but she would figure it out.

Because Chalmys was hers, and that was never going to change.

A glow settled around them as he tapped a crystal on the wall. With a soft click, a door opened, and Holly glanced into the room on the other side. No glowing god, though. She followed Chalmys through, expecting to find *something* special. But aside from a round crystal that seemed to have been discarded on a table, there was nothing of note.

After Chalmys touched the crystal, the response was almost instant. "Ah, I feared you wouldn't bring them. Good."

Holly jumped at the unexpected voice, but her stalwart mage merely glared at it.

"You dare much, Vier," Chalmys said sharply.

To a god. Either this was a strange world, or he was stronger than she knew.

"This isn't my fault," the voice countered. So smooth, that voice, and ridiculously melodious. Well, he was supposed to be a god of bards or some such. "The council is uneasy about the child you have there."

"Me?" Violet squeaked.

Holly took a step to the side, putting herself in front of her daughter where she curled against Chalmys's side. It wouldn't do any good against an actual deity, but even providing a distraction so the mage could carry Violet to safety was better than nothing. "It's okay, sweetie," Holly whispered over her shoulder.

Chalmys didn't look away from the stone. "We've already discussed this. I'm certain you reminded them that I have done no wrong."

"Yes, well." The god fell silent for a moment. "You're right, but they don't care. They've ordered the three of you to appear at the stone circle at noon tomorrow so that the council can confirm the child's good health. I was told to summon all three of you so the mother could be prepared."

"Prepared for *what?*" Holly cried.

Suddenly, the voice echoed in her head. *"If you are being mistreated, you may bring forth your accusations then in safety."*

Her mouth dropped open. "You have to be joking."

"I wish I were," the god continued aloud. "Listen. If you're anywhere close to unlocking Chalmys's story, now would be an excellent time to do so. You'll have the entire pantheon's attention."

"Oh no," Violet moaned, her face half-buried against Chalmys's shirt. "A bunch of gods? But I didn't do anything wrong. Did I? Maybe it was the flower. I plucked a secret flower, and now I'm going to be sent to a castle with a big beast. And no unicorns."

Chalmys rubbed the child's back. "You did nothing wrong, dear one. And I'd destroy any beast that tried to capture you. That's not a risk, though. Children are beloved here, so the gods merely want to make sure you're being treated well in this world. You'll only need to step into the circle and say hello."

Based on some of the fairy tales Holly had heard, that wasn't necessarily a bad thing. Hadn't the fae once stolen human children? Yet she hated the thought of being questioned by this weird council—and hated worst of all that she had no story yet to give Vier. She couldn't possibly write that in less than a day.

"Tell them Mr. Chalmys is the best," Violet said firmly. "Are you the one who stuck him here? You're mean."

"Violet!" Holly exclaimed, eyeing the stone. Not that she disagreed, but insulting an unknown god didn't seem like the best idea.

Chalmys laughed. "Hear that, Vier? You're mean. I hope you'll record that for posterity."

"If you weren't so—" The god went silent for a moment. "Forgive me for being mean to *Mister* Chalmys, young one. I give my word to be the height of kindness tomorrow. As for you, my friend, I meant what I said about the story. If you're still holding back, stop it. Kleress can't become the crown prince."

Holly couldn't explain it, but she knew at once that the connection had closed. Maybe she was getting better at detecting magic? She must have been right, for Chalmys spun away from the table and strode from the room. In silence, they crossed through the workroom, and when he turned toward Violet's bedroom, Holly said not a word.

It was surely past her daughter's bedtime, but getting the child to sleep would be a difficult task after that much drama. Holly would have to manage it, though. She had far too much work to do. With a resigned sigh, she moved around Chalmys to the bathroom. Maybe a long bath would distract her daughter.

Once the water was ready, she returned to the bedroom to find Chalmys entertaining Violet with a glowing crystal he'd set to spinning over his palm. "Bath time," Holly called.

He dropped the crystal into her daughter's hand and smiled. "There. Keep that in your pocket, and even the gods won't be able to bother you. It'll keep your dreams safe, too. You remember what I told you?"

Violet nodded. "Hold it against my cheek and say unicorn three times fast, and it'll bring me back to my room."

"Good job, sweetling." Then he met Holly's eyes over the little girl's head. "I hope you don't mind me giving her the charm. I thought it might help her sleep."

Her heart squished just that little bit more. "No, it's great. Thank you."

One little charm, and Violet fell asleep far sooner than Holly had dared to hope.

CHAPTER 24

Holly worked frantically into the night, but it wouldn't be enough. She'd barely managed to create notes out of the second half of Chalmys's outline by midnight. It would be physically impossible to write that into a coherent story. For one thing, she wasn't a storyteller by trade. She'd dabbled in that kind of writing just like any other, but it didn't come naturally enough to help with a project like this. Even a professional would balk.

She set down her pen and rotated her wrist, trying to work the ache out of her hand. How would she even start? *Once upon a time...* But the fairy tale format obviously hadn't served well in the past. It allowed the story to become fanciful, though such tales had originally been cautionary. Modern audiences had lost much of that fear.

Maybe she was overthinking things. She only had to tell his story—the curse had no stipulations about style or quality, as far as she knew. So long as she wrote out the facts with just enough interest to hold a reader's attention, it should at least suffice. *Goodness knows I don't have any fancy language left in me this late at night.*

An hour passed, the time marked by the steady tick of pen swishing over paper. No, this was never going to be enough. She'd barely made it beyond his birth after all she'd had to write about his father's crimes. There was absolutely no way she would have time to write down thousands of years' worth of training, battles, and adventures, nor the years of captivity, with all their useless attempts at freedom.

Holly rested her forehead against the heel of her palm. Her eyes burned with exhaustion and suppressed tears, and her shoulders ached from sitting in the same position for so long. Dammit, that god had sounded so certain that Chalmys would need his story told before tomorrow. Unfortunately, she didn't have a god's endurance.

She heard the rustle of Chalmys's robes as he approached, but she didn't look up. "I don't think I can do it," she whispered.

His hands settled on her shoulders. "Vier may have his wishes, but he's to blame for his own worry. Come to bed, my love. We'll solve the problem in time."

She didn't want to. No, she wanted to pull off a miracle. But she also needed rest for tomorrow. Violet would be both scared and excited, so Holly would have to be on top of things to manage her daughter's behavior. Attempting to stay up all night for a task she couldn't even complete would be foolish.

With a sigh, she straightened. "Fine."

And she let him lead her to bed.

HALF AN HOUR BEFORE NOON, Chalmys worked his way around the stone circle, casting shields and safeguards just beyond the rocks. He'd heard that Earth deities were all-powerful, but that wasn't the case here. The fae gods might be immortal with immense magic, but that didn't mean they couldn't be thwarted. With the blood of Iperan in his veins, Chalmys could do that better than most.

Vier's curse had only worked because he'd rested its base on the primordial flow, a deep magic that even the gods couldn't really control. At least not for long. Chalmys could touch that ancient energy, but not well enough to sever the curse. However, that merely bound him here by the rules the gods had set out. Within his domain, Chalmys could deflect nearly anything that didn't rely on the old, wild magic.

By the time Holly and Violet joined him, he was ready.

The ladies both wore lovely dresses, and it was clear that Holly had taken extra care with her daughter's overall appearance. Violet's hair was smoothed down, the usual play-induced tousle nowhere to be found. There was no tiny, leftover smudge of jam from her toast at the corner of her mouth and no hint of the dust that usually would have accumulated from her romps through the gardens.

Her scowl, though, was all natural. "I don't think I like these gods very much," the little girl grumbled. "I want to play in my tower."

"Remember what I told you," Holly said, exhaustion and worry lining her face. "You can't insult gods, baby. I don't know what they could do to us over it. Anyway, they just want to check on you. It's like a special invitation."

"Maybe," Violet said, but it was clear from her tone that she wasn't convinced.

None of them were, but he understood why Holly had tried.

A few moments before noon, they stepped inside the stone circle. Chalmys tensed, his entire body on alert for the coming intrusion. It had been some time since he'd last been summoned by the council, but that sense of violation lingered. He would simply have to bear it, that unfortunate side effect of the gods enforcing their access to the circle he'd built with his own power.

The slice of pain in his head warned him seconds before the wavering images sparked to life. His stomach squeezed, threatening to force his sparse breakfast back up his throat. This was his weakest moment, those heartbeats when he struggled to contain his revulsion. It didn't matter that it was unintentional—since he couldn't leave, there was no other way. But seething anger helped him with his struggle for control.

The image of Vier solidified to something almost opaque, though the semicircle beyond him remained vague and wavery. Even in his anger, Chalmys could admit that they likely did that for his benefit. The less of their energy they poured through, the weaker the effects of their intrusion. It wasn't much of a comfort.

"I, Vier of the Word, will act as the speaker of this council, though any god may bring forth their concerns."

Violet's hand wrapped around two of Chalmys's fingers. "I'm scared," she whispered.

"Your gift?" he asked softly.

"This dress has pockets," she answered, her tone oddly reverent.

He didn't have time to find out why she sounded awed, but he could guess why she'd mentioned them.

"Chalmys," Vier snapped. "Do pay attention."

He stared at the god he'd once called friend. Today, Vier wore his ever-changing hair short, the light blonde color usually an indicator of happiness, but his eyes appeared to be lacking their usual spark. Was he thinner? For certain, he looked more time-worn than flippant or jovial. He hadn't been faking his concern over current events.

"We have attended as required," Chalmys said. "As I told you, Vier, the bard currently helping me with my story brought her daughter. They are both here willingly and may leave at any time. This hardly required such a terrible intrusion."

Vier's lips pinched together as though he was pained—or holding back something he dearly wanted to say. But a swirling motion from one of the other god-forms prompted him to continue. "As I stated, I'm a representative, not the one with a complaint. You must satisfy them, not me."

Them. It could have been one or all of the others, and their shapes were too vague for him to discern their identities. Chalmys wasn't aware of any disagreement or difficulty he might have with the council, though. At this point, he couldn't do anything to cause offense. Were they truly this concerned about the presence of a single child?

"I assume you will wish to speak to Holly and Violet to confirm my words, then."

Vier nodded. "They will both need to step forward."

Violet's grip on Chalmys's fingers tightened, so he bent down to whisper in her ear. "Don't be afraid. I can protect you even from back here, and of course, there's always your pocket."

He worried for a moment that the little girl wouldn't let go, but just as he glanced up at Holly for help, the child switched her hold to her mother. Unfortunately, Holly didn't look a great deal more confident. Fear glimmered in her eyes, so stark it cut into his soul, but she covered it quickly enough.

Then with a lift of her chin, Holly guided Violet forward.

HOLLY WOULD NOT LET her hands tremble—her daughter would feel, and that was unacceptable. Her knees, though? Yeah, those were decidedly shaky. There was simply no avoiding it, even after Chalmys had done his best to prepare her. He might say that the gods weren't omnipotent, but they might as well be to her.

She stopped a couple of feet away from the god Vier. She'd expected handsomeness, and she got it. Yet there was a lot less charm than she'd anticipated seeing from a god of bards. Shouldn't he be a natural entertainer, with charisma practically radiating from him like too much cologne? He disappointed there. In reality, he just looked tired.

"For the moment, Chalmys will be unable to hear you," Vier said.

Her gaze shifted from him to the wavering lights behind him. What did the other gods look like? It was impossible to tell, but that wasn't necessarily a bad thing. Maybe some of them were hideous by human standards.

"There's nothing I have to say that he couldn't hear," Holly said, hoping her voice was strong rather than quivery. "Chalmys has been nothing but kind to us. And he wasn't lying. I walked through the portal of my own accord, and my daughter accompanied me happily."

"That's right!" Violet said.

Her sweet, brave daughter. Even Vier's expression softened when he looked down at the little girl. "You are fierce in your protection. Bold for even a fae child, much less a human."

"Are you the mean one?" her daughter asked.

Holly wanted to bury her face in her hands. "What did we talk about, sweetie?"

"Sorry, Mr. God," Violet said. Then she ruined it by muttering, "It *was* mean, though."

"Shh." Holly squeezed her daughter's hand in warning, though she couldn't decide if she'd rather laugh or cry. Sometimes, her child was the exterior version of her own mental voice. "We don't really have conversations with our deities on Earth, so I apologize for any rudeness. However, I do believe we have the right to be upset. I am here to help Chalmys of my own free will, and this is disrupting my task. Worse, it's scaring my child. Your device can create Earth food, so it seems like you would know enough about us to realize how strange this would be for her."

And me, but she didn't add that.

Vier grimaced, and a muffled cacophony erupted from the glimmers behind him. Holly gave a passing thought for the eardrums of anyone in their physical council room. If fae gods had actual eardrums. Or used a council room.

The noise settled quickly, but when the answer came, it wasn't from Vier. "You believe you can tell Chalmys's story? Hah. You might as well take your child and leave, for he will never yield it all."

Holly frowned. That voice sounded female, so probably a

goddess. Well enough, but why did the goddess sound so smug? So happy? She hadn't been the one to curse Chalmys. That had been Vier, whose face was now hard with anger.

"Hush, Peorban," another voice commanded.

Oh, shit. That was the goddess his mother had served. The one who absolutely *had to know* who Chalmys's parents were. Peorban was delighted that he was bound not to tell because he didn't want to risk his mother's soul. What in the sick bitch was *this?* No doubt the goddess had insisted on "checking on the child" so she could discourage Holly.

"Is this sort of meeting required of everyone who has tried to help in the past?" Holly asked.

"You are the first," Vier confirmed, though she already knew. She'd only asked so they would have to admit it out loud. "Since Chalmys has been acting out of character, some on the council thought it best to investigate."

And by "some," he meant Peorban. *She must be worried that his change in behavior is because I'm getting close.*

"As you can see, my daughter is happy and healthy." Holly smiled. "I hope you're sufficiently satisfied?"

She couldn't understand the murmurs that filled the circle at that, but she recognized the tone of a debate. It didn't sound like a heated one, at least—more the kind where one person had to be talked out of being unreasonable. Maybe with a side of "that kid in class who insists on asking questions long after the bell rang."

She almost began to feel sorry for the exhausted-looking Vier. Almost.

Finally, the voices stopped, and Vier inclined his head. "We are satisfied with the child's health. You may step back with Chalmys."

Holly released a long, relieved breath. "Thank you."

Her back burned from the weight of their gazes as she and Violet returned to Chalmys's side, but she did her best to ignore them. She focused on Chalmys instead. At his lifted brow, she rubbed his upper arm to offer comfort. "They said they are satisfied."

She expected his expression to lighten, but his frown remained as fierce as ever. As she faced the glowing gods again, she swallowed against a ball of dread. He thought there was more to come, didn't he? From the solemn look on Vier's face, it was possible he was right.

"They are allowed no more than two weeks here," the god said. "So as not to stress the child. Do not disobey this command, Chalmys."

"No!" Violet cried. "Not because of me! Mama still has work to do."

One of the lights brightened, solidifying into the pale image of a woman. Chalmys's breath hissed out as though he was pained, but the sound was drowned out by the goddess's laughter. "I told you. Go home," Peorban insisted.

Holly couldn't make out the goddess's image very well, but her face seemed to carry the same smugness as her voice. "Why are you so certain I should?"

"*No one* will be able to tell the story of Chalmys's life," Peorban mocked. "Look at you. Your energy is—"

Her voice cut off on a strangled gasp, and an ominous rumble shook the stone beneath their feet.

"Violet," Chalmys said in a strained voice. "Your pocket. Now. Then remember what I told you."

Her little girl pulled the crystal out and slapped it against her cheek. "Unicorn, unicorn, unicorn."

Violet disappeared with a flash and a soft pop. Though Chalmys had told Holly what would happen, she still felt like throwing up. Her daughter was alone in the house. Safe, but alone and probably terrified. She took the little crystal from her own pocket and tapped it. Her little girl had made it to her room, and she looked okay. But why was she pulling toys out of her toy box?

She believes she's helping one of my spells," Chalmys whispered into her mind. *"But don't worry. The only actual magic will be her preoccupation."*

As the rumbling increased, he stepped in front of her, light gathering in his palms. Holly couldn't possibly stop her hands from trembling, not now.

This meeting was clearly going very, very wrong.

CHAPTER 25

$\mathcal{P}$ain crushed through Chalmys's skull with increasing intensity, but he had no choice but to act in spite of it. This wasn't a normal reaction. Peorban's anger shook the ground until even Vier had spun around to confront her. What could she have sensed to infuriate her so? Did she somehow know that they'd discovered the truth?

"How *dare* you," Peorban spat. "You unawakened swine. Who are you to link yourself to someone so exalted? He was *mine*."

"What are you talking about?" Holly asked.

Chalmys settled himself more fully in front of her. "Do gods go mad, then?"

The goddess's terrible laughter suggested that they did. "Too bad for you that it doesn't matter. You'll feel the pain well enough when she returns to her world in failure. You should have practiced moderation, Chalmys."

"I won't fail," Holly said, her hand settling on his waist as she looked over his shoulder. "I can tell his story. All of it. Including the role *you* have played."

Lightning crackled overhead, but it dispelled against the

shields he'd added. He cast another around Holly for safety's sake and prepared a counter spell in case of a true attack. More lightning sizzled across the sky. One little opening, and—wait. Though magic snapped overhead, it didn't appear to be coming from Peorban. She stared up at it with the same surprise as the rest of them.

Vier pivoted to face him, but this time, the god had a new glow about him. Slowly, a grin twisted his lips. "What did you say?"

"I can tell all of his story," Holly repeated. "Chalmys, can you summon my papers here? And the journal?"

A new kind of pain bit at him at the thought, but he nodded. Holly eased to his side, her palms upturned. Despite it all, he smiled at the faith she showed, one he rewarded with a flick and pop of magic. She shoved the fluttering papers against her chest, steadying the stack before lifting it high once more.

"I have every detail here," she said, her voice rising against the low rumble of thunder. "And Chalmys has given me permission to share them all. More than that, I *know* him. His honor, loyalty, and kindness. All the things beyond dry facts listed on paper. No one can tell you more about him than I can."

He wanted nothing more than to gather her into his arms, but he couldn't look away from the council. Peorban's attention had returned to them with force, as evidenced by her cry of rage. The goddess started forward, but at Vier's lifted hand, another god grabbed her arm.

Then suddenly, Vier began to laugh.

"I can't believe this," he managed around his chuckles. "You found the loophole, and you didn't even realize it."

As lightning spread from the middle of the sky toward the horizon, an uneasy feeling crept through Chalmys. He couldn't decide if it was suspicion or hope. "Explain yourself."

Vier swiped tears of amusement from his cheeks. "I cursed you to find someone who could tell your life story. *Could,* Chalmys. All this time, you've sent these dreams out into the human world, trying to have your story told. But all you had to do was search for the full truth and then *share* it."

Chalmys's vision went white, then red-hazed, with pure rage. That bastard had let him flounder for centuries. "How long until it's gone?"

Vier sobered, catching his meaning instantly. "The curse will completely shatter in about a minute, I imagine."

"I suggest you prepare yourself," Chalmys said.

"Friend, please." Vier paled. "We'll have this out later. You have to share what you learned. If there was ever trust between us, I urge you to believe me now."

The land vibrated beneath his feet, a different resonance from Peorban's anger. It was his—his connection, his control. Soon, he would be able to draw energy from beyond where he'd been sealed. He would be able to shatter the link and send this whole wretched council away from his personal circle.

Holly's hand wrapped around his wrist. "We have to share this, Chalmys."

Peorban shouted out a curse as he turned his gaze to Holly. There was so much sadness in his love's eyes—but resolve, too. At the sight of it, he banked his anger as best he could. She was right, and as much as he hated to admit it, so was Vier. He had to reveal the truth about the goddess and Kleress.

"I will crush her," Peorban threatened.

For a moment, pain stole his breath, but at a comforting squeeze from Holly, Chalmys stiffened his spine. "I am the son of Prince Kleress and Larah, a priestess of Peorban's. Peorban allowed Kleress to use coercion magic on my mother in the middle of sacred rituals, and so I was conceived."

Peorban froze. "Th-that's a sick accusation."

"It's all in her journals," Chalmys said, tipping his head toward the bundle Holly held. "She wrote a confession to the high priestess and even continued doing rituals as she bore me. Do you no longer appear when your priestesses give tribute? Or did you watch Kleress rape her and then ignore her while she suffered in your name?"

Only thunder filled the air for a moment. Even Vier stared at him with wide eyes, and he'd already suspected some form of blasphemy. Then the god glanced back at the council. "I found another young priestess once. She killed herself after making a similar claim of coercion."

If there'd been silence before, it was impossible to keep up with the rumble of voices now. More gods solidified until Chalmys's head became darkest agony. All the while, his heart warred between lightness at the confession and terror for his mother's soul. Would she suffer? He couldn't bear it if she suffered.

A hush fell—Iperan was staring his way. "I thought I sensed a kinship, but through Kleress? There has been no word of this."

"For my mother's soul, I have hidden the relation my whole life. I cannot say why Kleress also hid this truth," Chalmys said. "But I assure you, Great-Grandfather, that he knew. He helped my mother hide my birth and then sent us back to the temple."

Iperan frowned, his gaze flicking briefly to Peorban. "But a priestess?"

"During the new moon ceremonies," Chalmys replied, twisting the knife. "Usually your holiest day, correct? He chooses his victims himself, and not only from Peorban's temple."

The outrage that followed nearly covered the booming rumble of the curse's final crack. The sky dimmed, then blazed with light as the energy was abruptly released. Chalmys fought to keep his eyes open against the power rushing in. Connection. He'd forgotten what it was like to be this free. This joined to more than a tiny corner of their vast planet.

He blinked as the light returned to normal. Though the world stabilized, the gods' argument had only begun.

"How could you allow such a thing?" Iperan shouted at Peorban, who was trapped in place by the other gods behind her.

The goddess hissed. "How could you marry that horrible fae

queen and then *ascend* her? Now your daughter sits on the throne, her power an affront to all temperance. And what of me, your abandoned fiancée? There must be balance to that insult, as well. Which Kleress understands. Naturally, he must take the throne, but he has done his best to provide me with a replacement from your bloodline. One who *should* have been more loyal."

Holly gasped, and Chalmys's body went cold. Peorban had encouraged the abuse of her priestesses so she could have him as her own? His stomach clenched. "Yet you kept me trapped here?"

Peorban glared at him. "I have yet to give up on Iperan. You should have been safe, awaiting my pleasure, yet somehow you found a soulmate. Now you're attached. As useless as Iperan is. Kleress will have to redouble his efforts once he's king."

Before the other gods could react, Iperan grabbed the goddess by the throat. "You will do no such thing. Nor will my grandson's poison find its way to any throne."

The other gods murmured their assent.

"Kleress has powerful coercion magic," Chalmys interjected.

Iperan nodded his thanks. "You will receive reward and recompense in time. And Vier will have much to answer for if he knowingly cursed one of my blood."

Light flashed, and Iperan disappeared, Peorban still in his hold. The other gods milled around for one confused moment before they departed, too. Except Vier, of course. Chalmys scowled at his former friend. How dared the wretched cur remain?

"Chalmys, I never intended—"

"Leave," Chalmys snapped. It was the last warning he would give. "I suggest you avoid my presence for a solid century if you wish to avoid a battle, and there are no guarantees even then. Yes, I see why you did it. You, who could have convinced me with words instead of placing such a curse. Go, Vier. Make amends with yourself for your own rotten honor."

Vier flinched—but he didn't argue. Instead, the god bowed. "I will send word when your mother's soul is safe, if it isn't already with so many gods involved. And tell the child I'm sorry for being mean," he said.

Then he was gone, and the circle was fully Chalmys's once again.

"Is it...is it actually over?" Holly asked.

She glanced around the empty circle, now bathed in gentle sunlight rather than the glow of divine entities. Beside her, Chalmys slumped, and his arm trembled slightly beneath her hand. The magic he'd held in his other palm faded, so she slipped around so she could look into his eyes. They were so full of emotion that it was difficult to discern them all.

But the curve of his smile held a definite twinge of sadness. "For the most part, yes," he said. "The curse has been lifted, and Iperan will deal with Peorban and Kleress. But I'll have to wait for confirmation about my mother, and I don't know what will happen when this truth is revealed to the rest of the world."

"Are you...are you going to go find out?" she dared to ask.

Did she really want to know? Unexpectedly, he was free, and now she had an inkling of what that really meant. She'd been aware that he was powerful. She'd read and made note of his history. Yet somehow, it had never really hit her that he was the great-grandson of a *god*. He had divine blood, and what bit of fae she had wasn't even active. With all his vast power, why wouldn't he leave her to roam where he wished?

"In truth?" He ran his hand roughly through his hair. "Aside from ensuring my mother's safety, I don't care. I have other things I would like to pursue. Currently, the most pressing is Violet, who has finally given up on her noble mission to bolster my spells in favor of sneaking into the dining room to summon chocolate cake."

Holly's hand flew to her mouth. Violet. How could she have

forgotten her own child? She should have rushed to her room as soon as the danger was gone.

"Stop fretting." Chalmys pinched her chin gently between his fingers and dropped a kiss on her mouth. "You knew she was safe. And she's more so now, since my scrying is easier. Not that Violet will appreciate that fact when she's contemplating trouble."

He swept Holly against him, and between one blink and another, she was staring over his shoulder at the dining room wall. Behind her, Violet let out a little shriek, followed by a nervous laugh. Oh, yeah. She was going to be coated in chocolate cake. But there was too much relief in Holly to be angry about it.

"I can explain," Violet said as Holly turned in Chalmys's arms. "I did just what I was supposed to. I promise. I put my toys in a circle all around the room, and I danced around, and I sang every song I knew. Just like Mr. Chalmys said. And then I felt all the dark stuff go away. But that was hungry work, Mama. I was starving."

Cake covered Violet's chin and part of her cheeks, and her best dress had quite a few brown splotches. But Holly was more focused on her words. "Dark stuff?"

"Yeah." Her daughter lifted one shoulder. "I dunno how else to describe it."

Chalmys's lips brushed Holly's ear. "Her fae blood may be stirring. Yours can as well, if you wish it."

She shivered—both from the sensation winging out from her ear and his suggestion. Did she want that? What would it even mean? Maybe it would be awkward for him to consider a relationship with her otherwise. With his power and pedigree... It made no sense that he'd ever mentioned courting her.

"I meant no insult," he whispered.

She turned back to face him, and his arms slipped around her waist. "Would there be...? I don't know. Benefits? Risks?"

His eyebrows drew together. "It would extend your life immensely, which I would count a boon. There are other ways around your shorter lifespan, of course, but although a form of ambrosia does exist, it isn't always easy to acquire. One slip, and—"

Holly placed her finger over his mouth. "Why do you sound confused that I asked?"

"Mmph." Chalmys nipped lightly at her finger before answering. "Did you not hear what Peorban said? Part of the reason she was furious was that we're soulmates. I thought you would rather be alive to enjoy that state. Unless..."

Her breath caught. Soulmates? Was that why she'd felt like she'd known him forever? It *did* make sense. But at the same time, she was certain that couldn't be responsible for her feelings. It was him and not some nebulous spiritual thing that had won her heart. Surely, he knew that. She smiled up at his beloved face— only to notice his worried frown. What had he last said? Unless... Wait, unless what?

Oh.

"Unless nothing," Holly insisted. "I've thought of you as mine since..." Just in time, she remembered the little ears no doubt listening behind them. "Our first nap. Honestly, I didn't even process what the goddess said about that. I didn't need to. I already love you."

The tension seeped out of him, and his forehead lowered to hers. "Do you, then? As I love you, my heart. Say you will stay with me as my wife."

Shock froze her very breath. Could she accept? There was so much to consider. Like their different lives. Violet. Her family. Oxygen—she absolutely needed to remember that. She sucked in air as hopes and worries swirled in her mind.

"Mama," Violet said impatiently from behind her. "If you don't make Mr. Chalmys my dad, I am *not* giving you any cake."

Holly nearly choked on a laugh. "Well, how could I possibly say no now?"

Chalmys lifted a brow, and she nearly chuckled again until she saw the doubt gathering in his eyes. She lifted up on her tiptoes so she could whisper in his ear. "Yes. But I still want to see your idea of courting."

"I heard that," Violet called. "No backsies."

Both of them laughed, then.

"Don't worry, Holly." He kissed her, lingering long enough that she nearly forgot what worry was. "I'll be sure to court you every day."

Well, then. She would definitely hold him to that.

The End

Thank you so much for reading. If you love romantic portal fantasy like The Mage's Curse, be sure to try my other series, The Return of the Elves. You can find the series here: https://www.bethanyadamsbooks.com/books

Do you also enjoy steamy fantasy romance serials? Turn up the heat with my pen name, Willow McCain. The first season of The Fae Kings' Bargain is currently complete on Kindle Vella. You can find out more here: https://www.willowmccain.com/books

ABOUT THE AUTHOR

Ever since finding a copy of *The Hero and the Crown* in her elementary school library, Bethany Adams has loved fantasy, even subjecting her friends to stories scrawled in notebooks all through high school. Eventually, she decided to publish novels of her own. When not working on her *Return of the Elves* series, Bethany enjoys reading and playing video games.

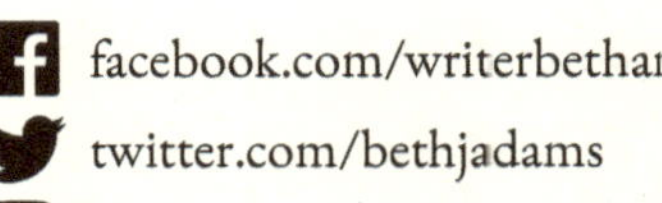 facebook.com/writerbethany

twitter.com/bethjadams

 instagram.com/willowreve

patreon.com/bethanyadams